Fatal ADDICTION

In the President's Service: Episode 4

Ace Collins

Elk Lake Publishing

Fatal Addiction In the President's Service Series, *Episode Four*

Copyright © 2014 by Ace Collins

Requests for information should be addressed to:

Elk Lake Publishing, Atlanta, GA 30024

Create Space ISBN-978-1-942513-19-3

Cover and graphics design: Stephanie Chontos

Editor: Kathi Macias

Cover Model: Alison Johnson

Photography: Ace Collins

Published in association with Joyce Hart of Hartline Literary Agency

To Alison

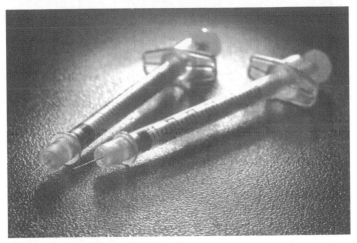

CHAPTER I

Sunday, March 29, 1942
12:22 AM
Outside of Brownsville, Texas

In a hidden spot on a hill overlooking the farmhouse, they waited. The moon was full and the stars were bright as Rebecca Bobbs' blue eyes followed the black DC-2 bumping down the dirt runway behind the makeshift tin hanger. Silently and fearfully she watched the airplane lift into the air, make a sharp left turn, and head south. In spite of having successfully completed her part of the mission, the forensic specialist felt like a complete failure. When it mattered most, her best friend's life was on the line, she was helpless, and it ate at her insides like a hungry virus. She wanted to scream, cry, and cuss all at the same time, but none of it would have done any good.

"Not good," Clay Barnes noted, understating the obvious as he pushed his lanky frame from the ground, dusted off the knees of his pants, and looked toward Bobbs. "Not good at all. She should never have jumped onto that plane. She's too impulsive, thinks with her gut and not her head, and I knew in time it would come back to kick her. The fact the DC-2 took off says all we need to know about Helen's fate. Henry was willing to die. He understood the risk, that it was a part of his job, and she should have let him do it. But she just couldn't resist playing mother or savior or whatever it was she was doing."

"It has nothing to do with being a woman," Bobbs argued, her tone almost hostile. "She did what you would have done if you'd been down there, but you're just too frustrated to admit it. We'd have all jumped in that plane to save him. That's what family does for family and, even though we just became a team, being a part of that team makes us family."

"But it was stupid," he snapped.

"If you'd been in her place, you'd have done it." She took a deep breath to bring her blood pressure down and then continued. "I just hope you're wrong about it being an impossible mission. Still, I'll acknowledge it won't take Fister long to find out they don't have Jacob Kranz. And once the charade is over, it pretty much signs a death sentence for both Henry and Helen. But, Clay, don't blame this on a woman's emotions; you'd have done the same thing."

"Maybe," the agent admitted. "But I sure wish it was me dying and not her. Boy, she had guts."

"You really think they're both going to die?" Dr. Spencer Ryan asked in disbelief as he rose from his stomach to his knees.

Bobbs shrugged. The doctor was a novice. He couldn't begin to comprehend the dangers involved in the split-second, gut-level decisions made in what amounted to combat zones. Until this moment he likely believed each adventure would be like a Hollywood movie, where the bad guys were quickly overpowered and the heroes took over the plane. As the craft headed for what appeared to be a fatal and fiery crash, they'd calmly discuss all they knew of flying, and one of them would somehow take the controls of the DC-2 and safely land it. If only it were scripted that way. While Helen and Henry could do a lot of things, flying a plane was not one of them. If anything happened to that pilot, her friends would be facing a rather ugly last few moments of life, and no scriptwriter was going to change that. It was time the rookie got that through his head. This was not fun and games. What they were doing was dangerous.

"Spence," Bobbs explained, doing her best to show no emotion, "Helen made a desperate move. Was it the right move? Anyone in the FBI or Secret Service would tell you no, but she did what she felt she had to do. No matter if we look at her as a hero or fool, we have to realize there's no way she could have gotten the draw on Fister. As much as I hate to admit it, Clay's right. She'd have been better off to just let the plane take off." The woman frowned. "She wasn't playing it safe from the time she left that house alone. Sadly, sometimes courage gets a person killed, and being a coward is often the key to living a long life."

"I've seen a lot of people die," the doctor noted as he tried to come to grips with the situation. "Had them die in my hands on an operating table. But I never saw someone willingly charge into death. And as someone whose life is dedicated to keeping hearts beating, it's hard to understand anyone doing what she did."

Barnes nodded, slipped his gun back into his shoulder holster, and glanced toward the young woman they had just saved. "Yeah, but you have to realize that Helen knew the risks. And as dumb as I think it was, she considered saving Henry Reese worth challenging those long odds." He shook his head. "We also need to remember that Helen's orders to us were pretty specific. If that command was her last act as the team leader, then we need to honor what she asked each of us to do. We can't do anything about what's going on up in the sky right now, but we can take Suzy back to her father. Once we get to Brownsville, I can also call the White House and see if they'll get the Army Air Corp involved in tracking down the plane."

"It'll be too late," Bobbs said.

"Well," Barnes shot back, "you don't sound much like little Becky Sunshine."

She shrugged. "Clay, you spelled it. Fister has them, and he'll enjoy eliminating them too. I want to get that guy someday."

"We both do," Barnes agreed. "But that day isn't today. Now let's get back in the car. Those guys down there who just watched the plane lift off aren't going to be in the dark much longer. They're going to figure out something is amiss when they discover Suzy's gone. We need to be four miles down that dusty road before all heck breaks loose down on the farm."

Pushing a strand of blonde hair off her forehead, Bobbs took a long, mournful look at the plane disappearing into the night sky before turning and hustling behind the other three toward the car they'd parked behind a small stand of mesquite trees. Only after she'd slipped in beside the girl in the back seat of the Ford sedan and Barnes started the motor and drove off the farm property onto the main road did she put voice to her thoughts.

"How many lives does a cat really have?"

"What are you talking about?" Ryan asked, his tone indicating confusion and frustration.

Bobbs looked first to the doctor and then to the driver. Barnes' face was colored a light shade of green from the reflection of the car's instrument lights. Though the glow was dim, she could easily see his skin was drawn and tight, his expression bleak. She didn't have to be a mind-reader to know he was just as sick about this as she was. But she also figured, even if he didn't answer, he understood what she was driving at. The only person who really needed an explanation was the doctor.

"Nobody I know," Bobbs explained, "has dodged death more times than Helen. She's made a habit of it. Clay even had to save her once, and Spencer, you had a hand in making sure she came through that assassination attempt. But this is a scrape I just don't see how she can get out of. I'm guessing she's on life number nine…as cats count. And, last time I checked, that's where it ends."

"Don't underestimate her," Barnes suggested. "A lot of folks thought they had Helen cornered, only to have her turn the tables on them. It wouldn't surprise me if that's what's happening right now on that plane."

Bobbs shook her head. He was lying for her benefit. He didn't believe for a moment that Helen had somehow gained control. And yet he forced a smile at her in the rearview mirror and pushed the conversation in a direction that provided them both with some sense of control.

"Out here, on this barren stretch of road, we can't help Helen or Henry one bit. Even when we make it to Brownsville, we have something on the agenda that trumps everything else. We have to make sure this young woman is safe. We have to relieve a father's fears. Those were our orders, and we have to follow them."

Bobbs nodded and glanced over at the young woman they'd freed. Suzy was small, pale, and obviously frightened, but she'd shown some spunk too. She'd survived an ordeal that would have reduced others to tears. And so far, there had been no crying. At this moment, even in the dark car, it was clear the kid's eyes were bright and her chin set. Hence, Bobbs was betting the coed would bounce back pretty quickly. Still, it might do the victim some good to share some reassuring words.

"Clay," Bobbs said, as much for the girl as for the driver, "no one's going to get Suzy again." She turned to face the victim. "Don't worry, young woman; your father will have his arms around you in a matter of minutes."

The college student nodded as she rubbed her hands and pushed back into the sedan's deep seat cushion. Even with her hair and clothing disheveled, she seemed strong and together.

She must have inherited some of her dad's grit. But while Suzy's problems were about to end, for the team there would be no sleep tonight. The real work was just beginning.

"Clay," Bobbs asked as she went back over the elements of the case, "beyond getting Suzy to her father and notifying the military about the plane, we have something else very important to do."

"Exactly," came the blunt reply. "Finding out what happened to Reggie Fister."

The words had no more than left the agent's lips when Suzy whispered, "He's horrible; he tried to attack me."

Bobbs' eyes once more met the girl's. Thoughts of Helen and Henry faded as the kidnapping took on a more ominous aura. Had Suzy Kranz been violated? Had the scum who'd nabbed her also used the girl in ways Bobbs didn't want to imagine? From what she knew of Fister, he would have relished taking away a young woman's innocence. He was completely immoral, merciless, and perhaps even psychopathic. Leaning close, Bobbs whispered, "Are you okay? Did he hurt you?"

"I fought him off," Suzy assured her, her dark eyes suddenly aflame. As the car bumped along the Texas back road at a mile a minute, she continued. "Dad would be proud; I left my mark on him." She paused, brought her knees up to her chest, and smiled. "My ring tore into his cheek. It'll take a while for that to heal. I bet there'll always be a scar."

Bobbs glanced down to the small diamond ring on the girl's right hand. The marquis-cut stone likely did do some damage, but Suzy's face was unmarked. So why hadn't Fister fought through it? Why had he just taken the blow and not struck back? What had stopped him? Perhaps nothing had. Maybe he had accomplished his hideous goal without leaving visible scars, and the girl was blocking that action from her memory. Even though she didn't want to pursue it, Bobbs had to find out. This was information Mr. Kranz needed to help his daughter recover.

"Suzy," Bobbs probed, "what did he do? Don't be afraid to tell me. It'll be best if you talk about it."

"He really didn't touch me," she admitted quietly. "But I could tell he wanted to. I could see it in his eyes. Those were evil eyes. It was like looking at the devil himself. After I hit him, he swore like a sailor and pulled his fist back to punch me, but the phone rang. After listening to the person on the other end of the line, he grabbed a couple of things and walked out. I never saw him again. So he never got what he wanted out of me. And he never will."

Suzy was lucky. If Fister had been given the chance, he would've made the young woman pay dearly for daring to challenge him. In fact, he'd probably have killed her. So what was that call about? Why did he simply walk away from what he obviously wanted so badly? It didn't make sense; it was completely out of character. He was, after all, a man who took pride in finishing jobs he started.

Bobbs leaned so close the two women's shoulders touched. Just loud enough to be heard over the Ford sedan's V-8 whine and the wind rushing through the partially open driver's window, she said, "Suzy, the Fister you hit was actually Alistar Fister.

He's Reggie's twin. He's the man who got on that plane with Helen and Henry. The real Reggie, the man we're looking for, was terrorized by the Nazis for years. He's confused, rattled, and coming down off drugs. He may look like the person who kidnapped you, but he's not vicious or amoral; he's a victim, just like you are. Do you understand?"

Suzy nodded.

Sensing the girl was grasping the concept, Bobbs continued. "We had Reggie with us this afternoon when we were planning how to rescue you, and he panicked and walked away. So he's not the one you have to worry about. If you see him, there's nothing to fear. Just look at his cheek. If it's not cut, you know it's not the man who grabbed you."

Barnes shot a glance over into the back seat. "Well, maybe not. But until I figure out why he took a powder, I'm not ready to admit he's just another victim. I think there's much more to this thing than we're seeing or you're admitting. I even believe they might be working together."

Bobbs didn't answer. At this moment, as she studied the college student to her right and thought about the fate of her friend and team leader, she questioned if being in the lab wasn't far better than being in the field. In the lab she never knew the victims, and crime was academic. There was no pain or suffering, no broken hearts, no sad eyes, no tears, no loss; there were only facts. Now that she was in the field, life and death had a very human and emotional context that shook her to the bone. And she didn't like it one bit.

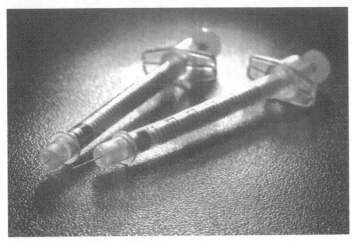

CHAPTER 2

Sunday, March 29, 1942

1:15 AM

Somewhere along the Mexican Gulf Coast

Helen Meeker was in a lousy spot and she knew it. It had been just over an hour since she'd defied logic and leapt on the plane. As the minutes and miles passed, all she could do was sit and study the gun the seemingly mute and obviously smug Alistar Fister held in his right hand. Thanks to a pint of her captor's blood, she'd recently dodged death, only to face her execution from the man who'd unwittingly saved her. There was a sick joke in that thought, but it sure didn't make her want to laugh.

Even though she wasn't tied up like Henry Reese, she was just as helpless. If she tried to charge Fister, he'd kill her before she lifted out of her seat. When Fister finally figured out that Reese was masquerading as Kranz, the gig would be up. The fact their captor hadn't yet picked up on the false identity sham was likely only due to the dim cabin lights. The situation wasn't just bleak; it was hopeless.

Perhaps in an effort to escape the reality of what she knew loomed ahead, Meeker pushed her legs against the plane's seat and thought back to her youth; of the tens of thousands of experiences and memories, the one she locked onto happened when she was nine. She was in vacation Bible school.

If, a few minutes before, she'd been asked what she most remembered from that summer week, it would have been good cookies and bad punch. But for the first time in years now, she recalled the "better than thou" attitude of Hazel Parker. Why had that memory resurfaced? Hazel was the preacher's daughter and played it to the hilt. The tubby little girl constantly pointed out all the ways the other kids sinned. She lived to spotlight failings. All through that week, Hazel smirked and gleefully repeated, "What you do in the dark will be revealed in the light." Now that thought finally had real meaning. When the lights came up, she and Henry would likely be facing not just the truth, but death as well.

"Thanks, Hazel," she murmured.

"What did you say?" Fister asked.

"Nothing."

Though the pilot didn't make an announcement, Meeker had no problem sensing the trip was almost over. As the twin props cut back and the craft begin a long circle, slowly drifting toward the darkness below, she wondered for a moment if Hazel Parker would find this situation amusing. Perhaps the child, now grown into a woman, would point her finger into Meeker's face and declare, "I told you so." Well, so be it. At least, if she died, it would be for something she considered noble and for a man who had real substance and value. That realization reminded her of another lesson from that long-ago Bible school experience: people became more like Christ when they're willing to lay down their lives for someone they love. Did she love Henry? She wasn't sure, but she was certain she liked him a lot. And going down with someone you liked was better than dying alone.

Knowing the end was near, she turned to her left and watched with tired eyes through a small oval-shaped window as the DC-2 gently set down on a deserted, sandy stretch of Mexican beach. Only after the engines were cut and the stillness of the night became apparent did anyone speak.

"I got you here," the pilot announced, his tone as flat as the ground on which they'd landed. "My job's over. It's up to you now."

Fister nodded as he glanced from the flyer to his captives. After eying Reese and Meeker, he grinned, ran his left hand over his smooth face, and ordered, "Turn your radio on. They'll probably touch base when they're here."

The pilot, his dark eyes fixed on the man calling the shots, frowned. "What do you mean? In the past we've always called them."

Fister stiffened, his face showing a hint of confusion before admitting with obvious forced bravado, "I'm new to this game. This is my first run. If you need to contact them, then do it. Let's get this show on the road. Hitler wants this package ASAP."

"Yeah," the man growled. "I'll do that."

As Meeker stared into Fister's seemingly pleased expression, the pilot switched on his radio and pulled the microphone up to his mouth. In a monotone he announced, "Black Wing to White Shark; come in, White Shark."

A few seconds later, a scratchy transmission could be heard over the plane's four-inch speaker. "White Shark here. What is your location, Black Wing?"

Helen considered the irony of being on Mexican soil with a pilot speaking English in a heavy Texas drawl to a boat filled with Germans, while a supposed English soldier held a gun on two American agents. If she hadn't been so sure these moments were her last, the situation would have been humorous.

"We're at the assigned location on the beach," the flyer explained. "Where are you, White Shark?"

As everyone onboard waited for the U-boat's reply, Meeker turned her attention from the pilot back to her smug captor. In that Bible school so long ago, it had been stressed time and again never to hate anyone. That principle had also been drilled into her at home by her parents. Yet at this moment, she couldn't help herself. She hated Alistar Fister. She hated everything he stood for and everything he was. She now wished she'd killed him when he'd almost assassinated Churchill and FDR. Why had she shown mercy that night? This man lived to inflict pain. He was evil incarnate. He was nothing more than vermin in human form. Fueled by sudden rage created by what she now viewed as her own stupid failures, she was about to leap from her seat when the faceless voice crackling over the plane's radio diverted her attention and calmed her illogical anger.

"Black Wing, we are just off the coast and ready to send a boat to your location to pick up the package."

The static-filled reply still hung in the air as Fister glanced from the prisoners to the pilot. He paused for a moment, looking like a cat trying to decide whether to continue to play with a mouse or break its neck, before saying, "Tell them to wait one hour."

"What?" the flyer shot back. "I have no plans to wait any longer than I have to. We always land, make the pickup or delivery, and leave. We do it quickly to keep from taking any unnecessary chances. I'll not stay here a second longer than needed."

"What's your name?" Fister demanded, his eyes locking on the now belligerent pilot.

"Vanderberg."

"Okay, Vandy, tell them one hour."

"If you think I'm staying here for one more hour, you're crazy. You're just asking to be caught. I value my skin too much to do something that stupid. Plus, we're dealing with unpredictable Nazis. They don't like to be kept waiting."

Fister pushed his gun toward the pilot's face. "I'm calling the shots. And now that we're on the ground, your skills aren't needed and your life doesn't mean a thing to me." He paused and grinned. "So you can either tell them to wait one hour, or you can die and I'll inform them of the delay. It's up to you. Is the chance of living until you're old and gray worth an hour of your time, or would you rather die young when your hair is still dark and full?"

"Why?" Vanderberg pleaded, showing no signs of backing down. "Why are you doing this?"

Fister laughed, his eyes shining. "I've something that needs to be done before Hitler gets Kranz. That U-boat can wait an hour and so can you."

The perplexed and angry pilot shook his head, frowned, picked up the microphone, punched the button, and announced, "White Shark, this is Black Wing. Package will be ready in one hour. Do you read?"

"One hour," came the almost immediate reply. "We will launch at 02:20."

"That is correct. Black Wing out."

Fister's eyes moved from the visibly upset Vanderberg to Meeker and Reese. He chuckled for a few seconds, seemingly proud of making the Nazi Navy wait, then casually leaned back in the co-pilot's seat.

Meeker shook her head. This was just like Fister. Knowing him, he likely would have her dig her own grave. Well, she wasn't going to give him that kind of pleasure. She wasn't a pawn to be used to entertain a sadist. She was a woman filled with pride. If he gave her a shovel and pointed to a spot in the sand, she'd swing the tool at his head and make him shoot her. If there were a grave to be dug, he'd be doing it.

As Meeker seethed and tried to come up with a plan to extract some kind of satisfaction from her last minutes on earth, Reese asked, "What's your game?"

Fister shrugged. "I enjoy making the rules and watching

others play by them. It's that simple. It gives me the kind of satisfaction that you can't imagine."

"Kind of like pulling the wings off flies?" Meeker asked.

"No," Fister assured her. "More like pulling the wings off pilots." The man in charge suddenly turned both his gaze and weapon back to the flyer and barked, "Give me the gun you have stuffed into your belt."

"Hey, now," Vanderberg complained, "wait a second. Why do you want it?"

"I'm a careful man," Fister explained. "I don't want you deciding to move the timetable up on me. If I have your gun, I have the power. And if you don't hand the pistol over right now, I'll kill you anyway. Remember, Vandy, I no longer need your services. That German sub is taking me back to Europe."

A now completely mystified Meeker, her curiosity aroused and her mind perplexed by Fister's unpredictable actions, observed the two men stare at one another for several muted seconds. During those tense moments, neither moved nor gave a hint they were going to give in. Finally, after Fister smiled and tensed the index finger of his right hand on the trigger, the pilot slowly brought his hand to his mouth. As he studied the pistol aimed at his head, he rubbed his lips and frowned. It seemed Vandy was as shocked by this turn of events as anyone.

"Death or life?" Fister asked, his voice as cold as ice.

"You're crazy," Vanderberg whispered.

"So I've been told," came the quick reply. "And, I will point out, you were crazy to take this job. You live in the United States, but you have no problems taking money for doing Hitler's dirty work. That's beyond the kind of crazy I am. And it also proves that no one on this plane, including me, can trust you. So I ask you again, would you rather be crazy or dead? You have five seconds to make up your mind. If you haven't handed that Smith and Wesson over to me by then, someone will have to go to a lot of trouble getting your blood out of this cockpit. Vandy, we're about to see what you're made of."

The pilot took a deep breath, filling his cheeks before pushing the air out through his lips. For a second it looked like he was figuring the odds. In the brief amount of time, he apparently realized they were all against him.

"You can have the gun," he announced. "I don't want to shoot anybody."

"Okay, Vandy. Are you right- or left-handed?"

"Right."

"Good to know. Use your left hand and retrieve your weapon. Move very slowly and grab it by the barrel, not the grip. You got that?"

"Yeah," the now wholly spooked pilot quickly replied.

"Then, after you have the barrel pointing at you and not me, hand it over. If it goes off accidently, I would rather it spill your blood than mine."

Vanderberg nodded and, using his left hand, slowly pulled the pistol from his belt, turned it around, and handed it over, butt first.

"Thank you," Fister replied as he flipped the gun over in his left hand and looked to Meeker. "Helen, would you mind holding this for me?"

Shocked and confused, the woman hesitated. What was he up too? What was his game? Why didn't he just kill them and get it over with?

"Helen, take the gun," Fister demanded, "and then you can untie Reese. We've only got an hour to work this thing out."

Meeker breathed a sigh of relief and smiled. Fister knew it wasn't Kranz beside her. That meant only one thing. "Reggie. How did you get here?"

"Rode out to the farm in the trunk of their car. I got in as they waited to pick up Reese. Once we arrived, I slipped out and, after everyone else marched Henry to the hanger, I followed my brother up to the house and watched through a window."

As Meeker took the gun, dropped it into her lap, and went to work freeing her partner, she asked, "So where is Alistar?"

"I don't know. He got a call, grabbed a couple of things, and went out the back door." As the ropes loosened and Reese pulled his hands free, Helen handed the agent the pistol. A moment later, a smiling Fister announced, "Your Colt is in the chair by the door."

Quickly pushing off the seat, Meeker hustled back to retrieve her weapon.

"What is this all about?" a now completely baffled Vanderberg demanded from the pilot's chair. "Have you gone stark-raving mad?"

"You picked the wrong side," Reese said.

"You're not Fister?" the pilot asked, looking at Reggie

"I'm one of the Fisters, but not the one you met earlier today."

"My Lord," an astonished Vanderberg announced, "you look just like him!"

"Yes. First time it's worked for me. Normally looking like him is what gets me in trouble."

Still amazed by the quick turn of events, Meeker moved to the front of the plane and glanced into the cockpit. "Reggie, I take it you have a plan."

"I'm not really into this spy game business," Fister admitted. "I just figured if we got on the ground, I'd get you two free and let you figure things out."

She smiled and moved to where her face was just inches in front of the still rattled pilot's. "Vandy, you're going to make a call. Get ahold of that sub and tell them that because of the importance of this package, your instructions say you can only turn Kranz over to the U-boat captain. You got that?"

"What if I don't?" he grumbled.

"Well then, as we're in Mexico and outside the jurisdiction of American law, you'll likely die violently and no one will ever find your body. How does that sound?"

"You don't mean that," he shot back. "You're a beautiful woman; you're not capable of killing someone."

"I've had very little sleep," Meeker stressed as she shoved her Colt deeper into the man's gut, "and I'm not an easy person to get along with when I'm tired. Besides, you're a mercenary and that makes you scum in my book. On the battlefield people like you are shot with no trials. We're at war, there's a Nazi sub out there in the Gulf, and you were going to put my friend on it. You didn't care what happened to him, and you wouldn't have blinked an eye or lost a minute's sleep if Mr. Fister had pulled the trigger and put me into the *big sleep*, so I don't owe you anything. Now, I think it's time you explain to your friends the rules of this exchange."

Vanderberg, sweat dripping from his brow, nodded. Seconds later, with Meeker's gun still jammed into his stomach, he made the call.

"White Shark, this is Black Wing. I have special instructions for you."

As the sub was not likely expecting the call, it took them a few seconds to respond. For the pilot, those seconds must have seemed an eternity. Relief flooded Vanderberg's face when he finally heard, "This is White Shark. What is it, Black Wing?"

The pilot looked to Helen. By now he had no doubt she meant business. When her eyes assured him he should continue, he pushed the button and added, "Your top ranking officer will need to sign for the package in person."

"Repeat."

Vanderberg took a deep breath. "I said, your commander must take the package personally. My instructions are that I'm not to give him to anyone else. Do you understand, White Shark?"

The transmission went quiet. As the moments dragged on, Meeker looked to Reese and Fister and shrugged. It was the FBI agent who broke the silence.

"What's the move?"

"Let's just say the charade's going to continue for a while," Meeker explained.

"You're going to take the officer prisoner?" Fister inquired.

"That's not at the top of my list. But I want that sub. So after we get this meeting locked up and finalized, and we get the man in charge away from the U-boat, the next call we'll make will be to our Navy. There's a base not far from here and, as I remember it, there's also an Army Air Corp group within easy reach of this site as well. They can get a fix on our radio signal and find the U-boat. At that point, they'll either capture it or blow it out of the water. Either way, it's big news both here and in Europe. With as many hard hits as we've already taken from the Japs and Nazis in the first few months of this war, we need some good news."

"Black Wing, this is White Shark. Directions understood. Herr Koffman will lead the landing party. What time is the pick-up?"

Vanderberg looked to Meeker.

"Fifty minutes," she announced.

The pilot repeated Meeker's instructions. After he finished, the communication was cut.

"That soon?" Reese asked.

"We've stalled them already," Meeker explained. "We can't afford to ask for anymore time without causing suspicion." She looked to the pilot. "Now it's time for you to move to the back of the plane. And Henry, while Reggie keeps an eye on Vandy, you need to switch frequencies and find a way to alert our military of what's going on. Let's hope they can scramble quickly."

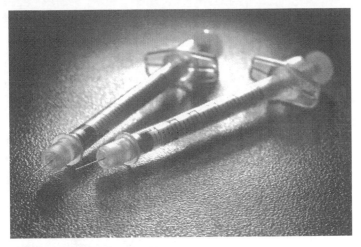

CHAPTER 3

Sunday, March 29, 1942
1:55 AM
Brownsville, Texas

Once they arrived at the hotel in Brownsville, Bobbs, Ryan, and Barnes turned Suzy over to her father. After watching the heartfelt reunion, the Secret Service agent and the forensic expert left the doctor with the reunited pair and moved quickly back to the all but empty hotel lobby. Stopping at the front desk, Barnes made a long distance call to the White House to set in motion a search for Meeker, Reese, and the raven black DC-2. As he did, a still alert Bobbs moved over to the business's front window and studied the moonlit street.

Brownsville had apparently rolled up the sidewalks. Except for a calico cat sitting under a corner streetlight, there were no apparent signs of life. She was about to turn back to check on Barnes when her sharp eyes noted a barely detectible movement.

Trying not to call attention to herself, she stepped back from the glass while staring into a shadowy area under a store canopy. After a few seconds to allow her eyes to grow accustomed to the dim light, Bobbs was certain someone was there, but who was it? Was it a man or woman? A policemen or storeowner? Maybe it was a drunk or a Mexican national or perhaps a teenager who'd snuck away from home. Whoever it was, they were doing their best to keep from being noticed. In the sixty seconds she'd been watching, the figure hadn't moved. If he hadn't been standing so close to the street, she might have figured him to be a cigar store's wooden Indian.

A car, slowly rolling down the main drag, gave her the break she needed. As the decade-old Pontiac sedan crept by the hotel, its headlights momentarily illuminated the individual in the shadows. Keeping her eyes on the form as long as she could, Bobbs moved to the front door and eased it open. Stepping out into the cool Texas air, she purposefully walked toward the Ford she and Barnes had used to escape from the farm. Opening the driver's door, she eased inside the vehicle, past the large, banjo-styled steering wheel, and scooted over to the passenger side. Once she was against the door, she reached into her purse, yanked out a compact, snapped it open, pulled it up in front of her eyes, and dabbed a bit of powder on her nose. As she did, she moved the glass until she saw the reflection of what was obviously a man waiting across the street. Thirty seconds later, she was still staring into the mirror and pretending to apply make-up when Barnes exited the hotel and wearily climbed into the sedan.

"I looked up and you were gone," he announced. "You need

to tell a guy before sneaking off like that." When the woman didn't reply, he continued. "Fine, ignore me. I was concerned you'd been grabbed by Fister. So don't just sneak off like that. We're a team; you need to act like you're a part of this. Anyway, the White House is alerting the Army Air Corp, the FBI, and the Mexican government to look for the black DC-2. I have no idea if this is good news or not, but no one in the media or at the FBI knows we're actually alive. So for what it's worth, our cover hasn't been blown."

She sensed Barnes' unrelenting glare, but rather than respond to his lengthy burst of information, she continued to stare into the mirror.

Evidently exasperated, he sighed. "Any idea on where Fister might be holed up? Or do you figure he's long gone by now? And why are you fixing your face at this time of the night?"

Bobbs dabbed a bit more powder on her forehead before whispering, "I think he's hiding in the shadows across the street. But don't look that way; I don't want to spook him."

Barnes sat up straighter, his voice taking on an urgent tone. "We need to take him. Who knows what that guy is thinking? He's either crazy or dangerous or both." He reached for the door handle and announced, "Let's move."

"Not so fast. I don't think he's recognized us. If he had, he'd be running right now. Let's see what develops."

As she noticed her partner hesitate, Bobbs glanced back into her mirror. Her timing was perfect. The man stepped just beyond the canopy's shadow and looked around. As a streetlight's glow hit his face, her identification was confirmed. It was Fister, and he was looking for someone or something. If she had to make a guess, she figured he was waiting for a ride.

"It's him," Bobbs said. "He looks like he's expecting someone to pick him up."

"Then let's move. We don't need him to get away."

"Hold your horses. Let me ask you a question or two before you go off half-cocked. Who'd be picking him up? How would Fister know anyone down here? And let me add, if you think both of the brothers are working for the other side, then this is your chance to prove it."

"How?"

"Easy. Let's nab him and his associate. We can't do that until that person shows up. It's simple math: one and one is more than just one."

"Becca, people do not sit in cars on city streets in the middle of the night. It's not normal. The fact we're not doing anything will soon tip Fister off that we're not to be trusted. So just sitting here we're bound to spook him. If we do that, we're likely to lose him too. So in the math of a person who knows something about common sense, a bird in the hand is worth two in the bush. Let's grab him and make him talk"

"Just like a man; you have no patience. You probably walk into a store and grab the first tie and shirt you see. Which is likely why you never seem to have as much style as Henry."

"I don't have style?" His feelings seemed hurt.

"No. You need to shop like I do. Go in, try things on, look for the right fit, study the colors and styles, and you might also look in a magazine or newspaper to see the current trends before even going into a store. Shopping isn't meant to be a knee-jerk experience."

"Women," he moaned.

"It's singular," she announced as she continued to watch Fister in her mirror.

"Singular?"

"I'm the only female here, so it's woman, not women."

He shook his head. "I still say we need to do something. This just looks odd."

As much as Bobbs didn't want to admit it, the Secret Service agent was right about the potential for drawing unnecessary attention by doing nothing. To stay in this spot they needed a reason for being parked on the street. And she knew of one particular cover that couldn't miss. Snapping her compact shut, she slipped it back into her purse, slid toward Barnes, and with no warning, reached up, put her right hand on the back of his neck, and pulled his face to hers. Just before their lips met, she whispered, "Keep your eyes open and watch him. And at least act as if you're enjoying this." She then pushed her mouth into his.

Bobbs could sense the agent's shock as they shared their first kiss. His body was tense, his lips tight and hard, his embrace cold, but he didn't stay frozen for long. A split-second later, he was enthusiastically playing along with the charade. In fact, he was acting more like a high school boy on his first date than a seasoned government agent on a stake-out. Once he relaxed, Bobbs quickly discovered the handsome single man was a good kisser—so good, in fact, that for a moment she almost forgot the purpose of this little act was to buy them some time.

Pulling back a few inches, she grabbed a quick breath and asked, "Is he still there?"

"Yeah," he sighed, sounding a bit disappointed. "And you're right; it's our man. He's not going anywhere, so we need to keep this cover going."

She didn't need an engraved invitation as she leaned closer and kissed him again. As her lips once more met his, she detected a hint of his aftershave. It smelled of powder, flowers, and a touch of spice. Why hadn't she noticed it before? And why had she never realized that Barnes had such wide, powerful shoulders? Suddenly she didn't care about his white shirts or boring striped ties.

"Okay," the agent whispered between kisses, "there's a light-colored coupe coming up the street. He's waving to it." He kissed Bobbs again before adding, "He's got something in his hands—a package, kind of round and long—and now he's getting into the car. We'd better get ready to tail him."

Bobbs reluctantly pulled out of the agent's arms and glanced to her right. The car's driver was a woman wearing a large, dark hat that obscured her face. As the Oldsmobile couple pulled away from the curb, Barnes started the Ford, waited a few seconds, and then steered the V-8 out into the street. Once he felt secure, he paced his speed with the Olds in order to keep enough distance between the two vehicles to not evoke any suspicion.

"Where do you think they're headed?" he asked, following their actions by making a slow right turn.

"I don't have a clue," she replied, her eyes moving from

the Olds to the man's face. He wasn't movie-star handsome, but he was good-looking. He had a solid jaw, a thin nose, and kind eyes. And he looked cute with his usually perfectly combed hair now falling down on his forehead. Had she caused that? And was she imagining a glint in his eye? Forcing her mind back to the task at hand but never taking her gaze from Barnes, she asked, "How much gas you got?"

"Half a tank."

"Okay, we can follow them for a hundred miles anyway." Suddenly a long trip appealed to her.

"It likely won't be that far. This is the same road leading to the airport we flew into earlier today."

"Catching a plane," Bobbs noted, "or maybe they have one chartered there. As late as it is, I'm betting on the latter."

As they drove along the city street, passing by long rows of small frame homes that the normally alert Bobbs barely noticed, Barnes kept his eyes and two hands on the wheel. Finally, after a couple of miles, he used his right coat sleeve to wipe the lipstick from his lips. Was this a sign he hadn't enjoyed or now regretted having to play their little game? Bobbs wanted to ask but didn't, for fear of both his response and the fact she suddenly wasn't sure about her own feelings. Taking a deep breath, she turned her eyes from the man to the Olds.

As Barnes pulled up to a stop sign, he eased to a halt before pushing the car into first gear and letting the motor pull the car forward. When he was through the intersection, he spoke, a tone of shyness in his voice. "That was a good plan you had, Becca. You showed you have the ability to think on your feet. We need that on our team. I had my doubts about you working as a field agent, but no more."

She nodded. "Yeah, that's what I was trying to do. You know, just coming up with a plan. I hope I didn't offend you or anything. I'd hate to come off as being that kind of girl."

"What do you mean?"

"By what?"

"That kind of girl."

She wished she hadn't said anything. How was she supposed to answer that question? Was she expected to tell the truth? Essentially, she was a novice in the matters of love. She had thrown herself into college and grad school, and worked full time in order to pay for it. Because of her demanding career and desire to prove herself in a man's world, she'd never really dated much. About all she knew of romance was what she'd seen on the movie screens. So how did she answer his query without coming off like some backwoods hayseed? Did she tell the truth or try to make herself out to be something she wasn't?

"I..." She paused as she toyed with a dozen different but equally unconvincing explanations. "I didn't want you to think I just fall into a man's arms at the drop of a hat. I mean, it takes more than dinner and a movie to get a goodnight kiss from me."

"How much more?"

So much for what she thought was a clever response. Now Bobbs really didn't like how this was going. She was completely out of control and painted into a corner. Worse yet, she'd supplied both the brush and the paint. As she rung her hands, he thankfully broke the silence and almost set her mind at ease. Almost.

"I know you're not that kind of girl. But…"

"But, what?"

He didn't answer. Instead his eyes darted from the car they were tailing to Bobbs and back. "Nothing." He smiled. "I guess we'll be working together a lot."

"Maybe. If the team stays together. Losing Henry and Helen tonight means they might break us up." The reality of that thought pushed her insecurities into perspective. Here she was acting like a high school girl with a crush when two people she deeply cared about might well be dead. How could she be so selfish?

"I hope they don't break up the team," Barnes mused as he dropped the Ford from second into third. "I think we have something special here."

Was he talking about the team or the two of them? A few minutes ago that wouldn't have mattered. But for some reason now, it did. Was it the kiss, or was it nothing more than a long, suspense-filled day? Maybe she was just tired or rattled. Maybe she was feeling fragile because of what likely was happening to Helen. Or maybe it really was the kiss….

"Could I ask you a question?"

Barnes' voice shattered her confused thoughts like a baseball flying through a stained-glass window. "Sure," she answered, fearing what he might ask and how she would answer.

"Bobbs is kind of a strange last name." His eyes continued to follow the car ahead of them. "I've never heard it before."

"Yeah," she admitted, relieved that was all he wanted to know. "It's weird, all right. But I wasn't born a Bobbs. Up until I was ten, I had a different last name. Kind of a dull story, one I'm not sure you'd want to waste your time with. Besides, it makes my family look pretty stupid."

"We have some time to kill while we tail Fister and that woman. We can either talk about your name or what more it takes to get a kiss than a dinner and movie. It's up to you."

"I think I'll feel safer with the name. Let's start out by saying the Depression was hard on my family. We moved a lot, and folks who moved a lot always drew suspicious looks. Or at least, it felt that way. Hence, we were always battling to gain trust." She paused. "I'm sorry. This really must be kind of boring to you. I mean, who cares about a bunch of Arkansas hillbillies trying to make ends meet? It's not the kind of thing that sells movie tickets."

He shook his head. "No, go on. Really, it's already a better story than I thought it'd be. Kind of hard to picture a sophisticated, stylish woman like you ever being a hayseed."

Did he say sophisticated? Did he really believe that? Is that how he saw her? In her mind, no matter how nicely she dressed, she still saw herself as that barefoot girl, wearing hand-me-downs and wishing she had a doll of her very own. Yet Clay saw her as a woman with style. Wow!

"Okay, you asked for it. I guess this is my version of *The Grapes of Wrath*. We started in Arkansas and kept moving west. Sometimes it'd be fifty miles, and other times a hundred and fifty. In my first eight years of life, I must have gone to a dozen different grade schools. Finally, after working at who knows how many different jobs only to have all of them play out, Dad found steady employment at a car dealership. They were impressed with his hard work and how quickly he learned things. That led to the Hudson Motor Company giving him a shot as a mechanic and sending him to Detroit to school. They told him when he completed his training they had a job waiting for him in Springfield, Missouri." She paused. "You sure this isn't boring you?"

"Better than listening to the radio," Barnes assured her. "Now what happened next?"

"We couldn't wait to move. We were jumping with joy and dreaming of buying new clothes and living in a house with indoor plumbing. Then Dad heard about a man who'd pulled several bank robberies in Missouri and Iowa. The man's name was the same as my dad's. The FBI didn't have a picture of the fugitive, but they put up posters all over the Midwest that had his name and description. From reading those, you'd think they were looking for Dad. Well, my father didn't want to be confused with the notorious robber, so before we moved, he went to court and officially changed our last name."

"That makes sense." Barnes pointed to the Olds. "They're slowing up a bit. I'm going to pull over to the curb by that gas station. The road's flat, the area open, and we can watch them while we're parked. After they get up the road a bit, I'll get back on the highway and follow them. And until someone comes up behind us or we meet another car, I'm going to keep the lights off. The moon's bright enough to see what's ahead." After steering over to the curb, he asked, "So, why Bobbs? Why not Jones or Smith or Kuzlouski?"

"Well," Becca explained, "My father was smart but not very imaginative. Our family name was Roberts. So he figured he'd just change it to what he thought was a short form of Roberts. What's sad is that my dad's first name is Bob."

Barnes grinned. "Bob Bobbs?"

"Yeah." She sighed. "And he was a big guy, so everyone always called him Big Bob. So I was known as Big Bob Bobbs' daughter, Becca Bobbs. Try living that down."

She glanced up the road. "You were right. They're turning into the airport. No commercial flights this time of night. They must have something waiting for them."

"I'll pull out and drive on by. That way they'll feel secure they weren't being followed. Once they're out of sight, I'll circle back and we'll see what's cooking." He grinned. "Big Bob Bobbs' daughter, Becca Bobbs."

She frowned. "Let's not talk about that anymore. In fact, let's never mention it again."

A few hours before she hadn't been the least bit scared of dying. If Helen hadn't ordered her to take care of the girl, she'd have charged into gunfire to save her friends. But a few kisses had somehow changed her attitude and resolve. Maybe it had been meant as a charade, but suddenly it seemed like so much more. Now her mixed-up emotions had caused her to share something she'd never told anyone else. Why had she opened up so much, and why did it suddenly seem she had so much to live for?

CHAPTER 4

Sunday, March 29, 1942
2:20 AM
Mexican Gulf Coast

True to their reputations, the German were prompt. They pulled their dingy up on the beach at the prescribed moment. The stoic man getting ready to greet the Nazi shore party wore a pilot's leather jacket, dark slacks, and a St. Louis Cardinal baseball hat. As he observed the Nazis pull their small craft onto the sandy, deserted shore, Reggie Fister wished that he, Meeker, and Reese had been given a bit more time to prepare. After all, the ink on their script was still not dry, so much of what they'd planned would have to be adlibbed and that was not Fister's forte. He was a by-the-book Scotsman. But ready or not, it was time to put the hastily pulled-together plan into motion. In this case, success depended upon the Nazi landing party not knowing him. If any of them recognized him as Fister, their entire plan was in big trouble. The only thing that could possibly save his tail would be some outstanding shooting from his two confederates. As dark as it was, how good could their aim possibly be? Suddenly what had seemed a good idea a few minutes before now appeared to have little merit.

Standing to his full six-feet height, his broad shoulders high and chin forward, Reggie walked out from beside the black plane and down toward the Gulf. His face displayed neither a frown nor a smile as he did his best to imitate how he thought Clark Gable might handle this scene in a film. Stopping a few yards from the obviously suspicious German sailors, he stopped, letting his black dress shoes sink a bit into the sand as he pushed his hands into the flight jacket and nodded. The visitors seemed nearly as apprehensive as he was.

"Koffman?" Fister asked, his voice surprisingly strong and steady in spite of the fact his heart was pounding like a kettle drum and his knees were shaking like leaves in a strong wind.

"Yes," the uniformed man answered. "And you are?"

"Does it matter?" Fister replied, doing his best to sound like a Texan. "Welcome to Mexico." He forced a grin. "The food is wonderful, but I'd stay away from the water."

The blond Nazi officer adjusted his hat, glanced over to the DC-2, and announced in surprisingly good English, "I'm guessing you're the pilot."

"That's why I wear the leather coat," Fister added with false bravado. "And by the way, I like yours as well. Nicely cut! Wouldn't want to trade, would you? I've always said the German military knew how to dress. Of course, that might not be the best sign. The Confederate Army had some very snazzy uniforms as well, and look what happened to them."

"You Americans," the German grumbled. "Always trying with the jokes. That attitude will cost you the war. I'm not here for laughs; I'm here to do business. Where is the package?"

"Mr. Kranz gave us a bit of problem," Fister explained, his eyes never leaving those of the man now standing at arm's distance in front of him. "As a result, he wasn't able to walk out with me. In fact, he can't walk at all."

"You killed him?" The German's face contorted in a rage that made him look almost like the comic-style Nazis decorating so many Hollywood movies.

"No, I didn't," Fister assured him. "But I was forced to put him to sleep. I don't think I hit him that hard." He glanced back toward the plane as he continued. "He likely won't be out very long, but I wouldn't be surprised if it took a while for him to get his sea legs. I polished my right hook in a lot of bar fights on both sides of the border. Those who are smart don't challenge me, and he wasn't too smart."

Koffman still didn't look pleased. Crossing his arms, he spat into the sand and mumbled something under his breath. As he did, the moonlight caught the reflection of a shiny, dark leather holster holding a silver-plated pistol. It was likely not just a fashion accessory.

"Listen," Fister explained as his eyes moved from the gun to the man's face. "I'm like the fisherman who guarantees his catch is both fresh and alive. In this case it only matters if he's breathing, and you'll be able to see for yourself that he is. Your two men can drag him back to your dingy with no problem. In fact, you'll be lucky because he won't be fighting you every step of the way. He's a feisty one, so in a way, I did you a big favor. I'll guarantee he'll wake up before noon. If he doesn't, I owe you a drink. You pick the bar and the time. Now, just so I satisfy your needs, I'm sure you can identify Kranz. I wouldn't want you to think I might pull a con. So let's go up and take a look at him."

The U-boat commander, his thin face silhouetted in the moonlight, glanced back to his men at the raft and then once more to his host. "I assumed that you would verify it was Kranz. I only know he is in his forties and a thin man with dark hair. I've never seen a photograph of him."

Fister smiled at the man who was at least four inches shorter as he yanked his hands from the pockets of what had been Vandy's leather coat. Thank the Lord, Meeker had guessed right. The Germans went into this assuming the package was the right one. It never dawned on them there might be any kind of deception, and to this point no one seemed to recognize Fister. From here on in, the plan should be easy.

"Gentlemen, if you will follow me back to the plane, I'll give you your package."

A now relaxed Fister, feeling more like Clark Gable than he had a few minutes before, spun and, with the three Germans following behind him like baby ducks, moved toward the DC-2. Leading the Nazi seamen over to a spot just in front of the plane's nose, Fister pointed to a figure on the ground. "I believe this is who the Fuhrer wants as his house guest. You can check him over. My right cross might have buckled his knees and taken the wind out of his sails, but I think you'll find him well enough for Hitler to enjoy torturing."

Koffman yanked a small flashlight from his coat pocket and shined it on the unconscious man's face. He studied it closely before stooping down to check for a pulse. Seemingly satisfied, he rose and turned back to Fister.

"There was supposed to be another man. His name is Fister. Where is he?"

Reggie snapped off his well-rehearsed explanation. "He didn't want to join the party, so I put a bullet in his head. As he was doing nothing more than taking up room on my plane, I pushed him out the door over the Mexican desert. I'm sure the vultures will be picking his bones by sunup. I can give you the directions if you'd like to go look at him, but it would be a pretty good hike even for members of the master race."

Koffman's jaw twitched. "My instructions were to deliver two men back to Germany, but your stupidity has now made that impossible. And you have the gall to joke about it as if it doesn't matter."

"You got the one Hitler wanted," Fister said, flashing a smile so large it revealed almost all of his teeth. "The other guy wouldn't have offered the cause anything anyway. His usefulness was up. Besides, he wasn't good at following orders. As I saw it, he wasn't really the model Nazi. He seemed a bit more of a Scotsman to me. And we know how unpredictable those people are. It would take at least a dozen Scots to take down a man like you."

The commander, his light eyes shimmering in the moonlight, glanced back to his men and then to the Gulf. With a seemingly placid Fister looking on, he kicked some sand with his right boot and cursed. Finally, without turning around, the German announced, "You won't receive full payment."

"Kranz is worth the agreed price," Fister argued. "After all, we know that's the only reason you took this risky mission."

With no warning, the Nazi whirled while smoothly yanking his Luger from its holster. He waved it for a moment and then smirked. "I see no reason to debate these matters. I'll take Kranz, keep the money, and kill you. I deserve the bonus for taking the risk."

"Do you practice that move with the gun?" Fister asked with a chuckle. "Or does it come natural? Listen, I'm not stupid. I know who I'm dealing with. Why do you think I asked for the extra hour to prepare? I have two men stationed in the darkness, and their guns have been aimed at you since before you left your raft."

"You're lying."

"You want to find out the hard way?"

"Listen," Koffman hissed, "you're a traitor to your own country. Men like you are lone wolves. They trust no one. They can't or they don't stay alive very long. You're all by yourself, and on this occasion that makes you a dead man. Where do you want the bullet? In your head or in your heart?"

Fister didn't give an inch. "Let me explain something to you. I'm walking out of this alive. I don't care if you do. I'm also walking away from this with my payment in full. And if you die, I'll pull the cash off your body." He paused, tilted his head slightly, and smiled before posing an observation. "I've been dealing with Germans for years. You only have faith in what you can see. Thus, just because you can't see my gunmen, you can't believe they're there. But I can prove I'm the one holding a full-house, and you're the one stuck with a pair of deuces."

"What do you mean by full-house?" Koffman demanded.

"Nothing," Fister replied, surprised the naval officer didn't play poker. After slowly pushing his hands into the coat's leather pockets, he glanced beyond the U-boat commander to the two seamen. "The man on the far side behind you. Is he right or left-handed?"

"They are both right-handed. Why?"

Ignoring the waving Luger and Koffman's sneer, Fister calmly explained, "Because you're going to need them to carry Kranz back to the dingy for you. I wouldn't want to have Henry shoot the man's dominant arm. That might force you to actually do a bit of the work yourself. I'd hate for you to break a sweat." After locking in on the Nazi's foreboding glare, Fister lifted his voice and casually ordered, "Left shoulder, the man on the far side."

A split-second later, a shot rang out and a Nazi sailor screamed, stumbled backwards, and fell onto the beach. As the stunned commander looked back to his man, Fister coolly announced, "Don't worry. He's still in good enough shape to help you get your package back to the sub. But if you force me to play another card, the next shot will result in your not being buried at sea but on a Mexican beach." He grinned. "How do you like the sounds of the surf? Do the waves soothe you enough for you to want them rolling over you for eternity?"

The German remained too stunned to speak. It was obvious from his expression he was completely unsure what to do next.

"Now," Fister barked, "do you put your gun away or does the next shot catch you between the eyes? It's up to you. I really don't care either way."

Koffman watched his injured man roll over and push himself out of the sand. As the seaman staggered to his feet, blood dripping down his left arm, the officer's face turned ashen.

"You should try to get more sun," Fister suggested. "You look like a ghost. And if you don't do as I requested, you might be one too."

Once more facing his host, the dazed man lowered the Luger to his side and frowned. His body language showed him to be completely beaten. With no hesitation or apprehension, Fister reached forward and took the pistol. There was no resistance.

"This will make a nice souvenir, but I can buy a lot more in Mexico City with the money. Now turn it over."

This time the German officer didn't balk. He resolutely reached into a pocket located inside his coat and pulled out a wad of bills. He studied them for a moment before mumbling, "Your payment."

"It has been a pleasure," Fister assured him. "Now, I want to get out of here before it gets much later, so drag this package back to your raft. And remember, there will be guns pointed at your heads until you're far out onto the water. So don't look back. My partners have been known to kill turkeys from a hundred yards away on one shot. And you're much bigger than a turkey."

There was no more quibbling. Without speaking, the German seamen picked up their package and, with Koffman leading the way, hurried back across the sand to the dingy. Once there, they not so gently dumped their cargo into the center of the small craft, and the injured man took his place alongside the still unconscious Vandy. Then the commander and the healthy seaman pushed off the shore and began the long row back toward the U-boat. They were halfway to their destination when Reese and Meeker stepped out of the shadows.

"Not the ride Vandy thought he'd be taking," Reese noted. "I love irony."

"He'll never make it to Germany," Meeker said, "if that's any consolation to him. I wonder if he'll wake up in time to see the party we've planned."

The sound of airplanes caused the trio to glance to their left. It was almost time for Mexico to taste a bit of the Second World War. As they stood on the beach, Fister, Meeker, and Reese happily observed a dozen Douglas A-20s appear in the sky, the moon reflecting off their wings. As the engines' drone grew louder, they watched the Army Air Corp pilots adjust their flight pattern slightly to the east and head directly toward the surfaced U-boat. The German metal fish, bobbing like a fisherman's cork, never had a chance. The sub's alarms had no more than sounded when the first load of bombs dropped. A second pass wasn't needed as, within seconds of the first assault, the vessel shook, exploded, and split into two pieces. The commander, still a couple hundred yards away in the dingy, watched helplessly as his burning metal fish went down.

Fister smiled. "With his cruise cancelled, I guess Koffman will soon be heading back this way. Do you suppose he'll want a refund on his purchase?"

"We don't give refunds," Reese quipped, "but we'll see if we can find him transportation and someplace to stay for a while." He watched the German raft sitting in the water, its stunned occupants likely debating their next move. "Helen, you got your big fish. I think we can call that the catch of the day."

"Yep," she replied as she walked across the sand toward the Gulf. "Good acting, Reggie."

The Scotsman smiled. "Thanks. I rather enjoyed it, but I do have a favor to ask."

Helen studied the spot where the U-boat had disappeared under the salt water. She enjoyed the scene for a few seconds before asking, "What's that?"

Folding his arms, Fister grinned. "I'd like to keep Vandy's leather coat. I think it fits me rather well. Just wearing it for an hour makes me want to take flying lessons."

"The coat's yours. And I think, with the payoff, you have the money for the lessons." She made a motion toward the water. "Koffman's headed this way. Let's get ready to welcome him back to Mexico."

Fister ambled up beside her. "If you don't mind, I'd appreciate the chance to pretend I'm in charge for a few more minutes. I think it would be jolly to arrest this guy using his own German Luger."

CHAPTER 5

Sunday, March 29
4:14 AM
Brownsville, Texas

Parking their car on the street, Bobbs and Barnes stepped out into the cool, predawn Texas morning. After looking at one another and nodding, they sprinted between the airport's terminal and a large wooden hanger. Stopping in the shadows, they watched Fister step out of the passenger side of the Olds and stroll over to a parked one-engine Cessna. The plane was painted royal blue with the identification of G-1407 written in white on the fuselage.

"Good-looking ride," Bobbs noted as she stood next to the agent.

"The C-165 Airmasters are not cheap," Barnes whispered.

"What's the plan?"

After pulling his gun, the man explained. "When the woman

gets out of the car and walks toward the plane, we should be able to run out and take them. They apparently have no clue we're here. I don't see any weapons. In fact, Fister looks like he's out for a Sunday stroll in the park."

Lifting her pistol to a point beside her shoulder, Bobbs nodded. "I'll take the woman. But I don't see any reason for gunplay. Reggie Fister isn't really a threat. He's just a confused man."

"We'll see," the agent replied as his eyes locked on the mystery woman who had so far remained in the car. "If he's so confused, how did he manage to find a dame like that?"

Bobbs kept her blue eyes locked on the Oldsmobile. After adjusting her hat, the driver, her face still hidden, swung open the door and stepped out onto the concrete. The men Bobbs had worked with at the FBI would have called this lady well put-together. She had curves in all the right places, and her dress hugged each of them. Her walk looked practiced, like that of a model; her hips rocked back and forth, and her stride was long. Whoever she was, she seemed to be created to attract attention and had no doubt heard more than her share of wolf whistles.

The mystery woman had covered about twenty feet when, just as Barnes was slowly moving forward, a 1936 Ford station wagon, its flathead V-8 purring like a kitten, pulled around the corner and rolled to a stop between the Cessna and the terminal. Almost immediately, a small, energetic Hispanic man jumped out of the driver's side, spun around, and opened the rear door. Within thirty seconds, five nuns, dressed in their black and white habits, emerged from the car. It was much too late for midnight mass and far too early for a sunrise service, so what was going on?

For the moment there was no way to make a move without putting the new arrivals in danger or having Fister and the mystery woman spot the government agents. With this unexpected development, what had once seemed so easy and clean now had the potential to become a bloodbath. Bobbs glanced from the women to her partner. Even though his pained expression proved he didn't want to, Barnes pulled back.

"Great," he sighed. "Just what I didn't want; we're going to have a church meeting."

"You don't sound too happy about it," Bobbs whispered.

"I went to Catholic school. Nuns scare me."

"Nuns scare you?" she asked in disbelief.

"They carry three-sided rulers, and they aren't afraid to use them."

Bobbs grinned. She'd never pictured Barnes as the uniformed little schoolboy and certainly had never considered him to be a man with a fear of women dressed in religious garb. She leaned close and whispered, "It's called sphenisciphobia."

"What?"

"Sphenisciphobia, the fear of nuns. It's actually pretty common. So don't worry; you're not alone."

"Good to know. I suppose you're going to blab that fact to everyone. I can just hear you now, shouting out that Clay is scared of nuns."

"I won't say anything," she replied, "if..."

"If what?"

"You never talk about Big Bob Bobbs' daughter, Becca Bobbs."

"Deal. Now, be quiet. One of the dragon ladies is talking. We need to hear what this hen party is all about."

"They're probably very nice. I never met a nun I didn't like."

"You never met Sister Rosey. Now shut up."

A still-smiling Bobbs turned her attention back to their unexpected guests. It seemed one nun was the spokesperson for the group.

"Thank you, Pedro. Now, once you get the bags out of the station wagon, you can go on back to the convent. We don't need you anymore."

"But, Sister Margret," the little man argued, "your plane is not here yet. I should not leave you alone."

"The plane will be here soon," the tall, thin woman assured him. "Mr. Vanderbilt promised he'd come here right after he got his other job finished. Then he's going to fly us to Houston. We have work to do at a charity hospital."

"I don't trust him," Pedro argued. "His eyes reveal a dark heart. And I don't like his black plane. Black is the color of evil."

Barnes grimaced. "You can say that again. Look at those habits."

"Clay," Bobbs whispered as she pushed her elbow into his ribs, "be nice or you'll be struck my lighting."

"Better than being struck by Sister Rosey."

Both agents' eyes locked on the woman in charge; Sister Margret was obviously not happy. To make that point, she shook her head with such vigor that her white cornette almost took flight. "Pedro, I taught Mr. Vanderbilt when he was in grade school. He might have some wild ways in him, but he always gives to the church and flies us when we need to go somewhere."

The driver didn't continue the debate. Instead, he moved slowly to the back of the car, opened the tailgate, and pulled out five small bags. As the quintet of women watched, he placed their luggage on the tarmac, slid back into the old Ford, slammed the door, and drove off. Meanwhile, a leather-clad man climbed into the Cessna and fired up the 165-horsepower Warner Super Scarab engine. It seemed departure time was here.

Bobbs nudged her partner and pointed to Fister. He was carrying a long cardboard tube and helping the woman into the plane. "We have to move."

Barnes nodded, stepped out of the shadows, and jogged left to avoid the nuns. Unfortunately, two of the sisters noted the man and his gun, and their off-key screaming likely woke up everyone within three miles. It also alerted Fister that something wasn't right. After tossing the package through the Cessna's open door, he stepped back behind the plane and pulled a gun. Crouching, his eyes followed Barnes as the agent skirted the nuns. Frightened and panicked, the smallest of the quartet turned and ran. Five steps took her around the blue plane where Fister popped up and grabbed her. Barnes froze as Fister pulled the woman against him and aimed the gun at her head.

Knowing she hadn't been spotted by either the nuns or those in the Cessna, Bobbs slipped into the hanger and began to circle behind Fister and his captive. She'd just found a clear position where she might be able to squeeze off a shot when Sister Margret shouted, "Young man, what do think you're doing with Sister Mary?"

Fister yelled back, "Are you in charge?"

"Yes," the older woman replied.

"Then if you want to see Mary live to say another rosary, you get your sisters over here by this plane right now. And don't drag your feet."

Margret didn't bother arguing; she rounded up her flock and quickly marched over to the Cessna. Once there, they obediently surrounded Fister. There was no way for Bobbs to get off a shot now.

Over the motor's roar, Barnes shouted, "Fister, no one's been hurt yet. Drop the gun, come over here, and this thing can end without bloodshed."

With all Fister's attention directed at her partner, Bobbs moved closer. When she stopped, her gun pointed toward the fugitive hiding behind the nuns, she was only about a dozen feet away, though she still couldn't see his face.

Fister pushed his hostage up on the wing. "Get into the plane, Mary, or whatever your name is. If you don't, I'll shoot the bossy woman doing all the talking. Now, move!"

"Don't do it!" Barnes shouted.

"I know who you are," Fister shouted back as the petite nun edged toward the plane's door. "Clay, stay where you are and no one gets hurt. There are two guns aimed at the nuns on the ground. There is another aimed at the woman who's getting into the plane now. If you want these women to live, then you're going to let us go. Otherwise there's going to be a lot of red, white, and black on the concrete. And you and I both know God won't like that."

There was no way Bobbs could get a clean shot. And with the nun now in the plane, even if she did manage to bring down Fister, it would likely doom the innocent women around the Cessna. With nothing to gain, those on board would mow down the nuns like weeds in a field. There was simply no choice; she and her partner were going to have to let that plane and its occupants take off.

"You have to let the woman on the plane go," Barnes shouted. "I can't let you leave with her."

"Not your call," Fister spat back, as he quickly made his way up the wing and into the plane's cockpit. "You have no choice, and you know it."

Helpless, Bobbs heard the motor roar louder, observed the nuns scatter, and the blue plane quickly lurch forward toward the runway. Dropping her gun to her side, she watched the aircraft gain speed and finally lift off into the night. Shaking her head in defeat, she made her way to Barnes' side.

"Guess you were right," she admitted.

"About what?"

"It appears both the Fisters are working for the Nazis." She paused. "What do you think they'll do with the nun?"

Barnes shook his head. "Unless she can beat them to death with a three-sided ruler and fly a plane, my guess is they'll kill her. After all, she can identify the woman and the pilot. We can't."

Bobbs looked back to the stunned quartet of nuns whose eyes were fixed on the plane as it slowly drifted out of sight. If they knew any prayers deemed for rescue, they needed to start saying them now.

CHAPTER 6

Sunday, March 29
6:19 AM
Over South Texas

After the pilot put the Cessna down on an open stretch of prairie west of San Antonio, Fister grabbed the frightened nun's arm, yanked her from her seat, and pushed her out the door. She balanced on the wing momentarily before tumbling into the field. She'd barely gotten up off the hard, barren ground, torn off her blindfold, and moved away from the wing before the pilot turned the plane, pulled away from the spot, bumped down a long stretch of open prairie, and lifted off. A few moments later the flyboy made a course adjustment and headed the blue bird north.

"You really think it was wise to let her go?" Grace Lupino asked as she applied another coat of bright red lipstick. She paused and looked into the mirror of her compact case. "I mean, she did see you before you stuck that blindfold over her eyes."

Glancing east at the sunrise, Fister shrugged. "She was blindfolded from the time we took off. What could she have seen before that? And even before we put the scarf over her eyes, you kept your face covered with that big hat, so she didn't really see you clearly. Since all the nuns saw me and Barnes even yelled out my name, my identification was already made. So what could the nun we nabbed tell the agents they don't already know? No sense upping the ante by killing someone unnecessarily." He continued to stare at the horizon. "Still, there is something that really bothers me."

"What's that?" she asked, scarcely trying to mask her indifference.

"Barnes is supposed to be dead. He died with Meeker and a bunch of others in a plane crash. It was in all the newspapers."

"It was dark and you didn't get a close look at him. How do you know it was really him? It could have been anyone."

"He called out my name."

"There are hundreds of FBI agents that know your face," she pointed out. "It was probably just someone who looked like this man you're talking about. What was his name?"

"Barnes."

"This agent's name was likely either House or Shed." She laughed at her own joke. "You're getting spooky, Al."

"Don't call me that," he snapped.

"Okay, Alistar." She let the last *r* hang in the air before frowning. "You're not nearly the man you believe yourself to be."

He glared at her then turned his gaze back to the rising sun. He studied it for a few seconds and noted, "Looks like the Japanese flag. Imagine that scene here in Texas. The state is waking up to the symbol of their enemy."

She pulled off her hat and ran her fingers through her hair. "Some people don't have friends, only enemies. For people like that, every sunrise is scary. So is every sunset and every moment of each new day. They always have to look over their shoulders and wonder who's out to get them."

"Was that barb aimed at me? You trying to say I don't have anything but enemies? My lord, woman, Hitler thinks of me as a god!"

She raised her right eyebrow and suppressed a laugh. "If you'd gone back to Germany, they'd have killed you. They only want you for the blood that flows through your veins. You would have no more than stepped off that U-boat when Hitler would have ordered his scientists to drain the blood from your body and find a way to put it into the bodies of all those visions of Nazi perfection he calls the S.S. Don't kid yourself. To Hitler and the Nazis, you've never been anything more than an experiment."

"You're wrong. Hitler wanted Kranz so he could punish the traitor." He tapped the long cardboard roll resting in his lap. "And he wanted this package so he could possess something of great importance to the Allies. But I was the real gift. He wanted me for the special things I brought to the table: my leadership, brains, courage, and charm."

Lupino smirked. "Let me explain something to you. Hitler wanted you a lot more than he did those pieces of paper, or even

Kranz. Those won't help him win the war, but he figured your blood might. And that's where the laugh was on him. You're a freak, a pumped-up warrior that offers a demented man some kind of hope his crazy plans can succeed. If he banks on winning the war on something you have in your body, he's already lost it."

It was amazing how much her view of Fister had changed in just a few weeks. When they'd first met, she'd been fully captured by his combination of good lucks and confident charm. But in time his arrogance became more than she could stomach. Now it was fun to poke holes in the blimp that held the man's inflated ego.

"Why did you call me?" Fister demanded. "Why did you beg me to say here rather than go back to Germany? If you don't care about me, if you think I'm a freak, then why save my hide?"

She smiled, knowing her white teeth gleamed in the morning light. "Because you have something I want. Besides, there's nothing magical about your blood, and I really didn't want you to die the way you would have if you'd returned to Germany. I want to see you make your exit from this world in a far different fashion."

"What do you mean about my blood? I can bounce back quicker from an injury than anyone. Wounds heal in days, not weeks, and bruises go away in minutes. For all I know, I might be immortal. You're likely sitting with a god. And don't fool yourself; if I'd have gone to Germany, I would have been Hitler's right-hand man." He thumped his chest. "I might have even been the next leader, the perfect example of the Arian race.

I'm the man Hitler wants all Germans to be. I'll father a future race of super humans. You should be kissing my feet!"

This time she let the laugh escape. "That's a nasty cut on your cheek. It's bleeding again."

Fister winced as he reached up to touch it. Pulling his finger away and looking at the blood, he snarled, "That little—"

"That young woman you kidnapped exposed you. You're not healing any faster than any other man."

"It hasn't been long enough for my blood to work its magic."

Lupino shook her head. "When did you first discover the unique characteristics of your blood?"

"Three years ago," he said, his voice a mixture of ego and pride. "Sure wish I'd found out sooner."

"What about your twin, the real Reggie? Does he have the magic blood?"

"Of course not. I'm the only one."

She shrugged. "Don't you find it the least bit strange that you and Reggie are alike in every way but your blood? I mean, you're identical twins. You came from the same egg. Shouldn't your blood be the same too?"

Fister stared at Lupino but said nothing. For the first time she felt she had him exactly where she wanted. Now it was time to really shake him to his core. "Alistar, when did Bauer start giving you vitamin injections?"

"About three years ago."

"And there you go. There's nothing magical about you or your blood. Bauer's the magician. You're just one of his tricks." She stared into his eyes. "You want to hear more?"

"You're crazy. Bauer looked everywhere until he found me. He convinced the S.S. to let me join him. He knew I was special."

Lupino shook her head again. "You need to go out and spend some time in that field behind his farm."

"I've been there," Fister assured her. "I've walked it lots of time. I know that whole place like the back of my hand."

"Then go there and dig down about six feet in those fields. If you do, you'll find all the others who thought they were special. He gave them the injections too, but with them it didn't go so well. The lucky ones that survived were made mutes and now serve as his errand boys and hired guns. As long as they follow his orders, they live. The rest were simply executed or died." She shrugged as she turned her attention back to the Texas plains. "A few were like you. They had the power for a little while. And he used them too, just like he used you. But as he improved his formula, he ridded himself of the past experiments. That's why you were going back to Germany. He was giving you to Hitler to dissect. In exchange, Bauer would get diamonds or gold or cash. You were sold like an award-winning cow at some county fair. That should tell you a great deal about who you are."

"You have no clue as to who I am," Fister growled. "And you certainly don't know *what* I am."

Lupino didn't answer. There was no reason to belabor the point. He'd find out in time.

"We're over the farm," the pilot announced.

"Let's land," the woman ordered as she looked down at the neatly kept ranch beneath them. It was nice to return to a world where she could soon call all the shots.

"We're setting down on grass," the flyer noted, "so it'll be a bit bumpy on the landing. Make sure your lap belt is tight."

Lupino snapped the safety belt and casually watched as the plane circled and dropped to the level, unpaved piece of pasture just outside Austin. She showed no fear or apprehension as the Cessna touched down and no emotion as it rolled to a stop in front of a large white stone barn. After the pilot tossed the door open, she climbed out, stepped to the ground, smoothed her red suit, and put on her black hat. She stared at a small herd of white-faced cows until she felt Fister behind her.

"Where to now?" he asked.

She turned and smiled. "I'm going to Washington. I have songs to sing and fans to greet." She reached out and took the rolled cardboard package from his right hand. "I don't really care where you go."

"Hey, wait a minute! You took me off my assigned mission, got me here, and now you're just going to leave me? You promised me something special, and I figured—"

"I know what you figured," Lupino replied with a sly smile, "and I don't give that away. Meanwhile, we're pretty close to the campus of the University of Texas. The local authorities now know about the kidnapping. Witnesses can describe you, so if I were you, I'd travel by night." She turned from Fister to the pilot. "Ralph, pull the plane into the barn. Before you take it out again, paint it and change the I.D. numbers. And, like always, don't tell anyone about me."

"Hey!" Fister yelled, reaching out to the woman, grabbing

her arm, and spinning her around. "You work for Bauer. We're on the same team. He'd expect you to get me back to him."

She laughed. "He was sending you to your death. Do you think he cares about you? But if you somehow make it back to Illinois, you'll have a chance to meet your replacement. I think you'll be impressed. Then he'll kill you."

"Why you—"

"Take your hands off me, Alistar," Lupino ordered. "If you don't, Ralph has a gun and will take your head off. At least alive, you have a chance to escape."

Fister glanced over his shoulder to the pilot and confirmed the woman wasn't bluffing.

Pulling away, Lupino strolled toward a waiting 1938 Graham Blue Streak. As she covered the dozen yards to the tan car, she heard a horrible groan behind her. Turning, she noted a confused, pained expression etched deeply into Fister's face. His eyes rolled back in his head, and he began to tremble. As his body tensed, he fell to his knees, his right hand clutching his throat, his breath coming in shallow gasps. A few seconds later, spasms tore through his body and he fell, face-first, into the red Texas dirt.

"What's going on?" the pilot asked.

The woman grimaced. "It's starting."

"What's starting?" Ralph lowered his gun to his side.

"Bauer calls it rejection. Like all drugs, each dose has to be greater than the previous one to have the desired effect. In time it turns toxic. That's why he was shipping Fister back to Germany. He wanted them to believe he had the answer to creating some kind of super-soldier and blame Hitler's scientists for messing it up."

"Is he dying?" the pilot asked as he watched Fister continuing to roll and shake.

"The drug builds up and in time begins to affect the body much like epilepsy," the woman explained. "He'll come out of it. When he does, put him in the barn and let him sleep for a while. Then give him twenty bucks and tell him to get lost."

"But will this happen again?"

"He's a dope addict. Just a different kind of drug than what we're used to seeing. He's got to have more of it or he'll go into a withdrawal like you can't begin to imagine. At this point, Bauer always puts his experiments out of their misery. I was at the farm one time—I was taken there blindfolded so I couldn't find it again—but I met Bauer and he explained his work to me. In a way, Fister's lucky. He's not going to be executed. He'll get to spend his last few weeks or months free. But I don't think he'll enjoy that freedom, and I doubt he ever charms another woman."

"But what about the seizures?"

"To my knowledge, this is the first. There'll be more, and they'll get worse. With scum like this, I almost regret not seeing him suffer again and again and again. There's a special joy in watching him not have any control over his life. But I have other things to do."

She turned on her heel, opened the door, and slid behind the Graham's steering wheel. After starting the motor, she paused to check her make-up. She was reaching into her purse for her compact when she heard a special news report form NBC blaring from the car's radio: "Overnight, off the Mexican Gulf Coast, the Army Air Corp spotted and destroyed a German U-boat. The Coast Guard reports that no crewmembers survived the attack. Eyewitnesses stated the Nazi sub was so unprepared for the American onslaught that no Army planes were hit by antiaircraft fire, and none of our planes was lost."

Lupino looked down to the cardboard tube and smiled. Now, not only would both Bauer and Hitler be convinced Fister was dead, but they would also believe the documents had been destroyed. Things couldn't have worked out any better.

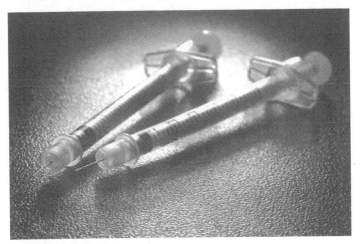

CHAPTER 7

Sunday, March 29
4:05 PM
Brownsville, Texas

The Army Air Corp pilot landed the DC-2 at the airport and taxied it over to a metal hanger at the far edge of the field. As Becca Bobbs, along with Clay Barnes and Dr. Spencer Ryan, looked on, the plane's door flew open. Without waiting for the steps to be put in place, Helen Meeker, her suit torn and her face dirty, jumped out. Becca gasped and felt her eyes widen. A few seconds later, Henry Reese, still sporting his theatrical make-up, joined his partner on the concrete tarmac.

"How in the world...?" Bobbs rushed over to hug her best friend.

"Long story," Meeker assured her as they embraced.

"Guess you heard about the German sub," an obviously stunned Barnes said as he reached out to shake Reese's hand.

"We watched it go down," Meeker answered. "In fact, it

was Reggie Fister who was most responsible for that little party."

"What?" a shocked Bobbs demanded. "We tracked Fister to the airport, and right on this very spot he got away in a private plane. That was early this morning, and we haven't been able to track that aircraft down yet. It's like it vanished into thin air. And now you're telling me Fister was helping you? That can't be. No man can be in two places at the same time."

"That wasn't me you were watching," a tall, good-looking man dressed in a leather jacket announced from the plane's doorway. After he stepped down to the ground, Fister joined the spirited band beside the hanger. "I took my brother's place at the little tea party back at the farm, and had a spot of fun playing the part too. Yet, while it's true I was the one who managed to disarm the pilot, it was Helen who came up with the plan that led to sinking the U-boat. It was jolly fun, I must say. Still, if we're handing out medals, she deserves the biggest one."

Bobbs' and Barnes' eyes jumped from Fister back to Meeker. Their confused expressions told their state of mind better than any words. Finally, as if a light had been switched on, Bobbs smiled and nodded. "Of course; this Fister has no gash on his face. If I'd gotten a close look at the other Fister, I would have known."

"So," Barnes noted, "we were actually chasing the dangerous Fister, and you all had the crazy one."

"I resent that," Reggie snapped. "I prefer the word eccentric. It's a revered Scottish trait."

"When did Reggie become such a character?" Barnes asked. "I think I liked him better when he was confused and subdued."

"It's the leather jacket," Meeker explained. "At least that's my theory. Now, what's this about Alistar being injured?"

Barnes gave a quick explanation and then said, "So this Fister is on the level?"

"He saved our lives," Reese admitted. "I believe he's passed the test."

"And," Meeker said, "I think we'll add him to the team. Of course, I'll have to get the president's okay on that. But having someone who looks just like the enemy could give us a big advantage. I think we can all agree on that." She tapped her foot on the tarmac, crossed her arms, and sighed. "Still, this whole trip has left me more confused than ever."

Bobbs frowned. "What do you mean?"

"We came down here to save a girl whose father Hitler wanted," Meeker explained as she looked at each of those gathered. "The Nazis had a sub waiting to take Kranz back home. Alistar Fister was in the middle of all that. Yet the U-boat commander explained that Fister was supposed to go back to Germany with Kranz. Why? And if Alistar was a loyal Nazi, why did he duck out on going back to Germany? Anybody have any guesses?"

As the team leader looked from member to member, her eyes fell on the one person who had remained mute. "Doctor Ryan, does the cat have your tongue?"

"I had just come to grips with your being dead," he replied. "What life are you on, anyway?"

Meeker frowned, obviously puzzled.

"The cat thing," Bobbs explained. "I figured you'd used up

all nine by now."

"You did?"

"Clay said your jumping on the plane was the dumbest thing he'd ever seen."

Barnes waved his right hand. "I didn't put it exactly that way."

Bobbs pointed her finger toward the secret service agent. "No, you also added the part about how women were too emotional to actually make rational decisions."

"This is interesting," Reese noted.

Meeker, a puzzled and slightly piqued expression on her face, looked from Bobbs to Barnes before shrugging and moving forward. "Okay, my question is this: could Alistar be freelancing?"

"What do you mean by that?" Barnes asked.

"It just seems there's more at work here than a Nazi plot to kill Churchill and FDR. Fister was not on a suicide mission. He was planning to escape that night, not die in a hail of gunfire. And then, when plans didn't work out and we caught him, he was sprung from the train and the real Reggie dropped in his place. I don't see how Hitler could have done that. From what we know, the Nazi spy network in this country isn't very strong or well organized. Yet Alistar has had constant help at each step of the way. So have I underestimated the Nazi reach, or does some other group have that kind of power?"

"Is that a question," Reese probed, "or do you have a theory?"

"Whose side is organized crime working on?" Meeker

asked.

"Their own," Barnes noted.

"Men without principles," Meeker explained, "work for those who pay the most. Last time I looked, our government wasn't paying organized crime anything."

"Do you think Hitler is?" Reese asked.

Helen fixed her eyes on Reese. "How about Mussolini?"

Bobbs raised her eyebrows. It was obvious Helen had been considering this possible connection for a while. "Can you link that up?"

"No," Meeker admitted. "I have no evidence, at least not yet. But Mussolini always maintained connections to organized crime. And there have long been connections between gangs in Italy, Sicily, and the United States. Mob leader Lucky Luciano has even offered to connect us with those syndicates in order to help protect industry and shipping. Maybe Fister really works for them."

"I'd have to see real evidence to believe that," Barnes declared. "This sounds like comic-book stuff to me."

Meeker smiled. "Who has the money, power, and resources to steal gold in huge volumes and get the two most important documents in the world?" She paused before adding one more nugget. "Henry, who tried to kill you, Becca, and Alison in my apartment?"

The FBI agent toyed with his fake beard before answering. "The gang that tried to kill us was made up of known hit men almost always employed by organized crime."

"And," Helen suggested, "if Hitler ordered the hit, does

that mean he's already linked up with the crime bosses? Or if Hitler isn't a part of it and it was Fister who called that shot, does that mean he's a part of the mafia or works for the man atop the organization here in the U.S.?"

"That's such a crazy idea," Barnes blurted.

Bobbs pulled herself together and responded at last. "Just like a man—no imagination."

Barnes raised his eyebrows, looking offended. "What do you mean by that?"

Bobbs stared at Barnes for a few seconds before replying. "You do know that all shades of blue don't go together, right?" Before he could answer or even dissect the question, Bobbs turned from her partner to Meeker. "Do you have any idea as to the identity of the woman who helped Fister escape?"

Helen frowned and shook her head. "Afraid not."

Reese addressed Bobbs then. "Didn't you get a look at her?"

"Not really. Some scary nuns blocked my view."

"Scary nuns?" Meeker's face showed her confusion. "How can nuns be scary?"

Bobbs shrugged and looked to Barnes. Meeker studied the glance between the two before asking, "Is this some kind of inside story?"

"In a way," Bobbs admitted. "But on a more serious note, Fister took one of the nuns with him. He may have killed her. In fact, I figure he likely did."

"Have you alerted the local police about the missing nun?" Reese asked.

"A phone call was placed to be on the lookout for the

woman," Bobbs explained, "but not by us. As we're supposedly dead, I thought it best the other nuns provide the sheriff with the information."

"Being a part of the living dead," Meeker noted, "has its advantages and disadvantages." She paused and looked over at Clay. "Can you fly this crate?"

"Sure," Barnes replied.

"Okay, then this will be our ride home. Let's go to the hotel, pick up our stuff, and get back to Washington. We've got an operations base to set up and some gold to find." Meeker licked her lips before adding, "And I also want to find Alistar Fister and make him pay. Trying to kill me or even the leaders of the free world is one thing, but targeting nuns and a college coed really gets under my skin."

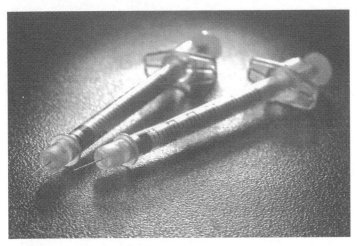

CHAPTER 8

Monday, April 6, 1942
5:30 PM
Two miles south of Litchfield, Illinois

Alister Fister had been on the move for eight straight days. Starting in Texas, he hopped a series of freight trains north. He'd manage to make the twenty dollars the pilot gave him last for half his trek. After that he'd been forced to panhandle or dig through trash. It didn't take long to discover the best offerings came in the cans behind country diners, though in those choice spots he had to fight alley cats for the good stuff. And he had the scratches to prove he'd bested the felines. Strangely, those wounds were no longer healing as quickly as they once had, echoing the warnings he heard from Grace Lupino on the plane. Was she right? Was he nothing more than a manmade freak? Had his whole life been a lie? The idea grew so deeply rooted in his psyche that every time he saw his reflection in a window. he halfway expected to see Boris Karloff staring back.

Just outside of Kansas City, Fister caught a ride on a coast-to-coast moving truck and, thanks to a beefy driver for Allied Van Lines, he made his way to Hannibal, Missouri. He spent two nights camping out along the Mississippi before opting to try his hand and thumb at hitchhiking. He struck out until he spotted a complete Army uniform hanging on a clothesline behind a rural farmhouse. As no one was around, Fister stole it, adopting the identity of a Private Willis. This simple change of clothing provided a sympathetic cover, and the rides now came quickly, as did offers to buy the "hero" meals. For the first time in almost a week, his belly was no longer complaining and he wasn't battling felines for scraps. But even while hunger no longer gnawed at his gut, there were still moments when he felt confused, disoriented, and helpless.

The blackouts happened with no warning and struck like a six-pound hammer. When he woke up, he could remember nothing. Though he couldn't be sure, he believed there had been six from the moment he landed in Austin until he finally made it to Illinois. The first must have lasted no more than five minutes, but each successive one was longer. The last one, by the river in Hannibal, left him unconscious for more than two hours. At least, that's how much time he'd lost according to his watch. What in the world was causing them? Did it have something to do with Bauer's injections? Or was it just a part of his physical make-up?

With so much time to think and reflect, the unsettling fits began to take on a sinister quality. Maybe God was making him pay for his sins, or perhaps Bauer truly had decided his project's usefulness was up. That would explain why the scientist planned to send Fister to Germany, where the S.S. doctors could try to farm his body for something of use in the war effort. Both the thoughts of blackouts and dissection sent chills up his spine and brought on dark, foreboding, and haunting nightmares. Every unexpected sound spooked him. The once fearless warrior even dreaded catching a glimpse of his own shadow. Had the injections not only affected his blood, but also supplied his courage?

The only way Fister felt he could once again become the man he used to be, the person who relished any challenge, was to face those fears. And that meant facing Bauer. But did once more meeting his mentor also mean he'd confront his executioner? If Lupino's story was true, then there was likely a grave in a field with his name on it. But wouldn't going out that way beat dying along the side of the road like a sick vagrant?

The shadows were growing long and a chill was invading the prairie air when a farmer in a large, beat-up truck stopped and offered Fister a ride. Even though he was dressed in a military uniform, the unshaven hitchhiker still appeared ragged. No doubt the old man dressed in a flannel shirt and bib overalls noticed. That was likely the reason he took a long look and posed a very strange initial question.

"You sick, boy?"

"Nothing contagious," Fister assured the driver. "But the Army sent me home for a while. They think it might be my heart or something."

"So they drumming you out?"

"Maybe," Fister lied. "Depends if I can get well. My uncle

has a farm just south of Springfield. I'm going there to rest up. Maybe I can get my strength back." Hoping his story rang true, he added, "Had scarlet fever as a kid. Maybe this is tied to it."

"Nothing like the farm life," the man assured him. "It makes a man healthy and gives you a good perspective on life too. I never lived anywhere but on a farm. My family's been farming the same land up north of Springfield for three generations. My name's John Links. According to your uniform, you're Willis."

"Yep. Steve Willis. I was born over in the UK but spent the last ten years in the States. Hoped to fight for the old red, white, and blue, but don't know if I can shake this thing." He paused, searching for a way to keep the conversation going. "I've never seen a truck like this. What kind is it?"

"Started life as a big old Pierce-Arrow sedan. When my Model-T died about five years ago, I found this thing, cut the back off, fashioned a bed, and the rest is history. Pierce-Arrows were high-dollar cars. Folks with money like the Rockefellers drove them. This is the best riding truck in the world. You know how you can spot a Pierce?"

"No," Fister admitted.

"The lights are mounted right on the fender and look kind of like lobster eyes. Nothing like 'em back in the 1920s, or even today. I think it gives this old beast character." He smiled. "Now back to you being in the service. Were you drafted, or did you join?"

"Found a line and got a uniform," came the quick and somewhat truthful reply. "Just wanted to fight for what's right. Didn't want those Nazis or Japs on our sacred land."

"Wouldn't have to worry about that if farmers ran the world. Heck, we treasure land and life too much to fight over it. We'd just meet at some café and find a way to work things out."

"You think so?"

"No doubt. You know, back in '33 I had a dispute with Ollie Simpson over a parcel of land to the north of my place. But we worked it out. You want to know how?"

"Sure."

For the next hour Links finished that story and shared others about his land, animals, and neighbors, as well as yarns about his childhood. During that time, Fister listened and nodded, only occasionally breaking in to give the man directions to Bauer's farm. Finally, just as Links finished talking about how smart his three grandkids were, they arrived at the destination.

"Thanks for the ride," Fister said as he stepped from the massive old vehicle.

"Take care. Hope you get to feeling well real soon." Right before he pulled away, Links observed, "Looks like your uncle's got a real nice place."

"State-of-the-art," the hitchhiker assured him.

Fister watched the man drive into the distance before cautiously making his way down the quarter-mile lane toward the two-story house. The last signs of daylight were fading, and night stars illuminated a completely clear sky.

Fister didn't bother approaching the front porch; instead, he eased his way around the house to the backdoor. He stood there for a moment, allowing the courage to build in his veins before raising his hand and knocking. He had no idea what to expect. If

Grace Lupino was right, Bauer might well shoot him.

After a few seconds, the door opened and a tall man framing the entry looked into the eyes of the pitiful creature on his stoop. He continued to study Fister for a few moments before finally breaking what had become a very awkward silence. His words revealed no mercy.

"I thought you were on a U-boat."

"Opted not to make that trip," Fister answered, his eyes not on Bauer's face but on his hands. When the man didn't reach into his pocket for the gun Fister knew was kept there, he continued. "Had a bad feeling about it."

"Your bad feeling was a good one; the Americans sank it."

"I hadn't heard about that," Fister admitted.

Bauer nodded but made no effort to ease the situation. Fister felt more like a bum asking for a handout than an associate of the man in the doorway. Maybe, considering his last eight days on the lamb, that's what he was—just another hobo trying to get through one more day.

Realizing Bauer was not inclined to ask any questions, Fister opted to make the next move. "It wasn't easy to get here. I bummed rides, grabbed food where I could find it, did what I had to. Even stole this uniform."

"Did you roll a GI for it?"

"No. I didn't have the strength to do that. Just took it off a clothesline."

"Alistar, you've slipped a long way in a very short time." Shaking his head, Bauer finally held the door open and stepped aside, allowing his unexpected guest to enter. "Go into the study;

we can talk there."

After making his way through the kitchen and down the hall, Fister entered the small, neat, book-lined room and nearly collapsed onto the couch. Still looking disinterested, much like a man forced to entertain an uninvited life insurance salesman, Bauer took a chair across the room. After lighting a cigarette and taking a long draw, he smiled, put his feet up on a stool, and crossed his ankles. At least for the moment, he didn't seem to be in the killing mood.

"Something's wrong with me," Fister said. "I'm having blackouts."

His host nodded. "That's to be expected. It's been a while since you've had a fix."

"A fix?"

"One of your shots. They keep you going. Without them your body just gives way."

"You didn't tell me that."

"No reason to. If you knew, you wouldn't have been nearly as good in the field. You wouldn't have felt immortal. And that's what you needed, to think you were a god. Of course, none of us really is a god, but a few, like myself, get to play god from time to time." He smiled. "And in the right circumstances, I find that's something I enjoy."

He took another drag on his cigarette, held it in for a moment, and then exhaled before continuing. "Let me share the difference between you and me. Men like you work for men like me, and they get dirty in the process. Sometimes they die. Men like me move people around like pieces on a chessboard. If we lose one or one breaks, we just get a new one. And don't fool yourself; we never mourn our losses. That's a sign of weakness."

Now Fister was sure Lupino had been right. Bauer was the one who had created him, and evidently created a lot more just like him. That meant the man Fister thought he was had been a lie; he wasn't special at all. Needing to verify what was now so obvious, he wearily lifted his head and asked, "The shots are what made me who I was?"

Bauer shrugged. "The injections, combined with your colossal ego, yes. But without the shots, your ego wouldn't have carried you far." After switching on a lamp, Bauer folded his hands and continued. "You've lasted longer than the others. Some died within hours of the first injection; others made it a few months. The guy I pegged to replace you had a heart attack after three days. That was a shock. He had the potential to be so much more than you were. He was smarter, stronger, quicker, and had a deeper understanding of the mission. In time he would have grasped my long-range plans. I might have made him my partner. He was so wonderfully immoral and obedient."

"I don't follow you. What were the plans? Aren't you just a cog in Hitler's machine?"

"You never did get it." Bauer grinned. "But I still believe if you hadn't let lust drive so many of your decisions, we could have accomplished so much more. You just couldn't get the ladies off your mind. Blondes, brunettes, and redheads were your Achilles heel. That's the problem with men; they always have weaknesses that others can exploit. At least, everyone but me."

"What's in the stuff you shot into me?" Fister asked, bringing his hands to his arms in a futile attempt to ward off a chill. "What does it do?"

"You really want to know?"

Fister nodded.

Bauer took another long draw on his cigarette and got a faraway look in his eyes. He stayed locked in on what must have been an old memory for several minutes before finally focusing once more on his guest.

"You know the story of Dracula?"

"Sure, but what does an old movie have to do with me?"

"I'll draw you a picture; see if you can follow it. The count constantly needed new blood to recharge his batteries. With it he was strong, but without it he was sick and old. I won't go into the details of what's in the drugs you were given, but I can tell you that once you started taking them, you needed them as badly as Dracula did blood."

After sucking more smoke into his lungs, Bauer exhaled and snuffed out the cigarette in an overflowing ashtray on the end table. Folding his hands over his chest, he continued. "I refined what Nazi scientists learned in the death camps, meaning that a lot of Jews died to make you what you were. In particular, the S.S. doctors worked on twins. They constantly toyed with them to find out what made them special. You were the answer to their prayers. You were a German twin with a Scottish brother, and they got you when you were still a young teenager. They had you in in their grasp early enough to create an environment where it was natural for you to be amoral and heartless. In fact, they encouraged it. They also built up your ego as they destroyed any regard for life other than your own. The process they employed is an almost foolproof way to create a killing machine."

"And you were a part of all of it?"

"No," Bauer said with a wave of his hand. "I had no part in your youth. But when I found out about you, when I visited the program and watched you in action, I was the one who came up with the plan for you to take your brother's place at school, on trips to the States, and even to appear to die in France."

"So you set up the plan that had me pretending to fight off hundreds of Germans. Those Nazis playing soldier that night were something you dreamed up and convinced Hitler to put in motion."

Bauer laughed. "Alistar, you still haven't figured it out. Those weren't Nazis who grabbed you that night. They were my men posing as Nazis. Only after I arranged that did I inform the Germans of my plans to use you to infiltrate the English command. Then everything broke right for something even greater until you messed up and didn't kill Churchill and Roosevelt. That's when I really started to become disappointed in you. Yet I believed I could still use you. But when you tried to kill Meeker, I realized you were becoming too hard to control. Then, even though you likely don't remember it, you had a seizure. Thus, I thought it was time to give you back to Hitler."

"So I'm nothing more than a piece of machinery," Fister lamented.

"You're a tool," Bauer admitted, "but that's essentially the way I think of all people. So don't take it personally or get your feelings hurt."

Fister sat in silence. What was this game Bauer was playing, and why did he have so much influence on Hitler?

"You said those weren't Nazis who set it up to make me look like a hero."

"No, they weren't."

"Then who were they?"

Bauer sighed. "It doesn't hurt you to know now, I suppose. They were members of a crime network that still thrives in Europe. I employed the same kind of men, this time Americans, when I helped you escape from that train in New York and let the FBI catch your brother."

"But you never told me how you knew where I was."

"Alistar, you poor dense boy! I have a mole in the FBI, in the White House, in the Fuhrerbunker, and even in Wolfsschanze."

Fister gasped. "In the Wolf's Lair?"

"Yes, and in a hundred other places you'd be just as shocked to know. But I get the idea this knowledge is secondary compared to what you really want to learn. You've travelled a thousand miles and endured a host of hardships to ask me something, so go ahead and ask it."

Fister hesitated then took a deep breath. "Am I dying?"

"I'd be lying if I told you anything else. What I injected into you made you as strong as a lion but likely also gave you about the same life expectancy." Bauer shrugged. "But wouldn't most men trade their old age for a chance to be…what is that comic character called? Oh, yes, Superman."

Fister shook his head and muttered, "I should kill you."

Bauer laughed. "You don't have the strength. But now that your planned replacement is dead, I might be persuaded to give you another fix and build you back up. Not sure how long it will last, but as I keep working on improving the formula and your body seems to take to it better than most, I might be able to give you some time. And isn't that what we all want?"

"You can make me like I was?"

"No guarantees," Bauer admitted. "But the odds are at least fifty-fifty that I can buy you some more time to feel invincible. So, if you're willing to take my orders, we can go to the lab and fix you up."

"What choice do I have?"

"None if you want to live."

Fister's eyes went to the floor. He wanted to live if for no other reason than to get revenge on two people. The first was Grace Lupino. He'd trusted her and she'd betrayed him. The other sat across from him right now. Lifting his head, he fixed his eyes on Bauer.

"If I agree, I need to know who I'm I working for."

Bauer's answer was simple and straightforward. "Me."

"But what about Hitler, the Third Reich, the Nazis?"

"What about them?"

"Aren't you with them?"

"Let me explain something to you." Bauer's smile was hard and wicked. "I don't care about flags; I care about power and money. While I seem to work with those who might be political in nature, they only think they have my loyalty. When this war is over, I will survive and thrive. Right now there are high-ranking officials in Washington and London who think I'm on their side, just like the crazy man in Berlin thinks I'm working for him."

"You're a double agent?" The thought was almost beyond Fister's ability to comprehend.

"Double, triple, or quadruple…what difference does it make? What I do isn't about the fight for worldwide conquest; it's all about souls."

"Souls?"

"Yes, Alistar, souls! In war, I'm setting in motion the framework to own a lot of the drug trade in this country and around the globe. And in my lab here, as well as my other facilities, I'm developing new forms of heroin and other hard-line drugs that are more addictive than any ever seen. But that's just the beginning. I'm also buying into the legal drug trade and food industry. I'm developing products that will create new, much more subtle forms of addictions. Think of this: power is having something people have to have and will pay anything for. That's what I'll provide to millions of all ages and stations of life, no matter who wins the war."

"You mean…?"

"You have no idea what I mean." Bauer's eyes glowed. "You need me right now and will sell your soul for the fix to make you feel like a superhuman again. And as badly as you need that fix, your drugs don't have nearly the addictive power of what I'm talking about. I want you think about this: take your need for a fix and multiply it by ten. Imagine what the businessman or the housewife would give for a fix like that. Imagine what the food industry would pay for an ingredient that made their candy or cereal that addictive. I could go on and on. But the products I'm developing will create an environment where people are unknowingly addicted to what seems like life's necessities. And once they're addicted, I have their souls." Bauer chuckled. "Then I take the money I earn from feeding their desires and plunge it into the market, banking, and business. I'll also buy politicians with my money. Imagine the power I'll have."

"That's impossible."

"No. What Hitler is trying to do is impossible. You can't rule the world with force. Armies can't maintain control of the earth for long. History is littered with those who tried. But desire can, and I'm going to be the force behind not just what people want, but supplying what they can't live without."

He paused and laughed. "It not about who wins the war; it's all about who wins the peace."

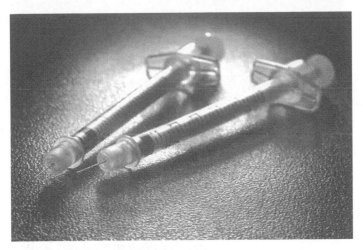

CHAPTER 9

Tuesday, April 9, 1942
9:32 AM
Outside Drury, Maryland

A century-old, two-story brick colonial-style house, located in the middle of a 135-acre non-working farm, well hidden from the road, was chosen as the headquarters for the team working in the president's service. The basement was quickly converted into a shooting range, interrogation area, and laboratory. The second floor of the huge old home provided six bedrooms, one for each member of the group. On the entry level, the living room served as a place to relax, listen to the radio, and read; the parlor became a library, the large ballroom a conference area, and the rest of the rooms kept their original purposes. The team took turns cooking, while Bobbs and Ryan, masquerading as a young married couple, fronted as the owners of the property. The least recognizable of the group, they used their cover to purchase supplies, retrieve the mail, and run outside errands.

Each detail of life was carefully worked out to cloak the real purpose of the farm. Private messengers delivered packages to the locked front gate, where a buzzer was rung and, after dropping off the goods, the drivers left. Only then did one of the team leave the house and retrieve the materials.

The team was given four cars: a blue 1939 Packard, a black 1937 Buick, and a maroon 1940 Ford Deluxe, all sedans, and a 1936 red Auburn coupe. Except for the Packard, which Bobbs and Ryan used on their trips, the other vehicles were kept in a large wooden barn. Also stored in the building was a 1938 Ford sedan delivery, outfitted with all the latest in surveillance equipment, and a 1942 Ford one-and-a-half-ton truck with a canvas-covered bed.

An almost hidden lane connected the barn to a small road at the property's rear. This allowed the team to come and go unobserved. Yet over the first days, they worked such long hours they barely had time to eat. It was only a visit from the president's personal physician — one of only two of their White House contacts — that caused all but one of the members to immediately pull back from organizing their work stations and take positions around the large, dark dining table. For a few minutes, the housemates and Dr. Cleveland Mills exchanged pleasantries until the final member of the crew appeared.

"Good to see you, doctor," Helen announced as she waltzed into the room, scanned the group, and then took a seat at the table's head. "What do you have for us?"

"Well," the older man began, "the U-boat's commander has

opted to spill a bit of information. It seems Fister was supposed to deliver a couple of documents to the Nazis."

Meeker, dressed in a light blue sailor-cut dress and flats, nodded. She knew the answer before she even asked. "And what were those documents?"

Mills scratched his brow. "He claims he doesn't know, and we tend to believe him. But I think it deals with why this team was formed."

"So," Bobbs cut in, her blue eyes almost flashing with excitement, "you believe they're the Declaration of Independence and the Magna Carta?"

"I think so. And if that's the case, then we pretty much know they're still here in the United States."

"And," Reese added, "it's not too large a leap to believe the Nazis were behind that theft and the gold as well." He stared at Meeker. "That pushes organized crime to the back burner."

The team leader shrugged. He was right—for now—but she wasn't ready to give up on the connection.

"Becca," Barnes asked from his position beside the doctor and across from Bobbs, "could the cardboard tube Alistar had with him contain those two items?"

Bobbs nodded, causing a bit of her blonde hair to fall over the right side of her face, covering her eye and temporarily causing her to look a bit like actress Veronica Lake. She pushed the stray blonde strand back. "The length was right. My guess is that Fister has it. Or at least, he had it when he left Brownsville."

"So," Meeker cut in, purposely disrupting what had turned into a two-person verbal dance, "finding Fister becomes the pressing goal. But where do we start looking? Intelligence has reported no sightings of the man since Clay and Becca last saw him."

"The nun they took as a hostage has been found," Mills announced.

Bobbs' eyebrows shot up in apparent surprise. "She's alive?"

The doctor nodded. "For whatever reason, they dropped her off on a wide open part of the prairie, about an hour west of San Antonio. A Mexican rancher found her walking across one of his fields. Since he and his wife didn't have a car or speak English and the nun didn't speak Spanish, they couldn't communicate much. It was a week later when a neighbor came by in his old Model-T truck and was able to translate from English to Spanish that he found out the story and took the nun to town."

"Have we interviewed her?" Reese asked.

The doctor smiled. "If you mean the FBI, the answer is yes. An agent named Collins spent a few hours with Sister Mary. Here's her description of the pilot, though she caught only a brief glimpse of him before being blindfolded." Mills glanced down to a typewritten sheet sitting on top of a manila folder. "He was white, somewhere between the ages of twenty and fifty, wore a blue baseball hat and large, dark glasses." The doctor looked across to Reese. "She had no idea of his height or weight and seemed to remember he might have had a mustache, though she wasn't sure. In her defense, it all happened so fast and she had only a split-second to take it all in."

"Not much to go on," Meeker noted.

"She did remember the woman called the pilot Ralph," Mills added.

"That makes it so much easier," Reese said. "All we need to do is find a pilot named Ralph who's somewhere between five and seven feet in height, could be fat or skinny, and is either barely young enough to vote or might have grandchildren."

"What about the woman?" Meeker asked, ignoring Reese's sarcasm.

"Basically," Mills explained, "the description matches what Bobbs and Barnes observed: dark hair and a big hat. About all the nun could add was that she heard Fister refer to her as Grace. And here's something else: when no one was talking, the woman passed the time singing pop standards, including *Blues in the Night*."

"The Dinah Shore hit," Ryan noted from the far end of the table.

"Good to see you found your voice," Mills quipped. "I thought you might have a touch of laryngitis. Okay, where was I?" He took another look at his notes. "Oh yes, the nun said the woman had a pleasing voice, wore a red suit, and had the whitest skin she'd ever seen." He looked up. "And that was it. She didn't have a chance to see anything else before she was blindfolded."

Meeker shook her head and frowned. Even Sherlock Holmes wouldn't consider this case elementary. She looked back at the doctor. "What was the town where she was dropped off?"

Mills consulted his notes. "Utopia."

"Utopia." Meeker took a moment to digest the name, and then got up and walked over to a road atlas placed in a bookshelf against the far wall. She picked it up, dropped the book onto the table, and flipped through the pages until she came to Texas. With Bobbs now beside her, Meeker found Utopia and used her finger to trace the route down to Brownsville. She glanced at her friend. "They were flying north-northwest."

"Playing it safe," Bobbs noted. "They avoided major cities and skirted San Antonio with all its military bases. Essentially, if they were going to land somewhere and drop off the nun, they would have gone west of San Antonio rather than east. There's far more open range, so it offers a lot of spots to land a plane."

Meeker nodded. "So where were they headed? Got any guesses?"

"Logic would tell them to go south to Mexico. But if Fister has gone rogue and is intent on selling the documents, then he had to travel where the money is. That means staying in the States."

"Keep going," Meeker urged her friend.

Bobbs glanced back at the location where the nun was left. "Okay, if they'd been going west, they would have followed the Rio Grande. If they'd wanted to go east, they would likely have hugged the coastline. I think they were headed north, probably to the Midwest, and were avoiding major cities with their flight plan."

"So you're saying they would likely have turned back north once they passed safely by San Antonio?"

"That's my guess."

"But where to then?" She looked down the table to Mills. "Any reports of a blue Cessna with the numbers Clay and Becca gave you?"

"Registration numbers matched a completely different plane in another part of the country. And no one knows of a blue Cessna anywhere."

Bobbs sat down and drummed her fingers against the table.

"You got something?" Meeker asked.

"Clay," Bobbs asked as she looked up, "you fly planes and know a lot about them. What was the model of the aircraft we saw that night? I remember you mentioned it, but I'm drawing a blank right now."

"C-165 Airmaster."

"Are they rare?"

Barnes rubbed his chin as if that would help his thinking. "Probably not more than eighty of them ever made. They were good planes, but too expensive. And the war stopped their production. I recognized the motor as the smaller of the two that went in the Airmaster, so the one we saw was likely built early in the production run."

"What's the plane's range?" Bobbs asked.

"In ideal flying conditions, maybe 450 miles. A good pilot could probably coax another twenty-five or so out of it."

Bobbs looked back to the map. "Okay, they likely couldn't have made it to Waco, so my guess is they would have set down in the Austin area. Once there they would have either switched modes of transportation—after all, they had to figure we'd put out an alert on the plane—or laid low. I'd bet dollars to donuts that Cessna is still in central Texas."

Meeker smiled. "Okay, Dr. Mills, we're all supposedly

dead, so you have to get into FAA records and see if there's a C-165 Airmaster registered to anyone in that area."

The doctor nodded, and Helen turned her attention to the secret service agent.

"Clay, you know planes as well anyone. Since we still have that DC-2 stored in a Baltimore hanger, why don't you fly back to Texas and start doing some interviewing? I'm guessing the plane we're looking for isn't registered at all or is registered in a different part of the country, but people have to have seen it. I think your being on the ground in that area gives us the chance to actually find the pilot. While I doubt Fister allowed the plane to take him to his final location, since he's too smart for that, I do believe the pilot might be able to give us a lead on the woman."

"I can leave today," Barnes assured her. "Why don't you let me take Reggie? If we track the pilot down, we might fool him into thinking Reggie is Alistar and have a better chance at getting the information we need."

"Good plan," Meeker agreed. "How does the range on the DC-2 compare to the Cessna?"

Barnes grinned. "Twice as long, and our black bird is a lot faster than his blue one. So if it comes to both of us being in the air, we can run him down or run him out of fuel. We win either way."

"Okay, I like those odds. Still, we've lost more than a week, and that gives Alistar Fister a huge head start. It's time we make up some ground."

The team leader turned to her longtime partner and lifted her eyebrows. "Henry, we need to make some connections in the underworld, find out if there's been any kind of talk of someone offering some very rare documents for sale."

"Got it. I've given Dr. Mills the names of agents who can help him."

"Spencer," Meeker said, "you've had your lab up and working for the past two days. Any progress on finding out what makes Fister's blood so special?"

"Not really, but I can assure you of one thing. It's not natural, or Reggie would be blessed with it as well. It has to be something he's either been exposed to, absorbed, or was injected with that works the magic. Based on the blood tests first done by the FBI and the blood we used on you, which was taken a day later, the abilities the blood had to —for lack of a better word— regenerate, diminishes pretty quickly. It's almost like a battery losing its charge."

Meeker nodded. "So you think he needs to have some kind of treatment on a regular basis to maintain his power?"

Ryan shrugged. "I think it's a drug that interacts with the blood when it's injected. I've invented a term for it. As the street name for illegal drugs is dope, I'm calling it blood-doping. Sure wish I had more of his blood for testing."

"I'll do my best to get you a whole cabinet full the next time I come face to face with the guy." Meeker looked around the room before pointing to the door. "Time's a wasting. Let's get to work."

As the men filed out of the room, Bobbs asked, "What about me?"

"Becca, you and I are going to take what little we know and

try to figure out who our mystery woman is."

"Any idea where we start?"

Meeker moved over to a window that looked out at the large, two-story white barn. Crossing her arms she said, "Alistar Fister was briefly in the United States several years ago as a student. As far as we know, that was the only time until he made the rounds in Washington as a supposed hero. If I had to make a guess, I'd put money on the fact he met the woman within the past few weeks. Either he charmed her and picked her up, or—"

"Or she works with the same people he does," Bobbs interrupted, finishing her friend's thought. "As we know nothing about the organization, we need to start looking for a stylish woman named Grace in the Washington area."

"And with as little as we have to go on, it would be *amazing* if we found her."

Bobbs laughed. "That pun wasn't worthy of you."

"It's a fact, not a pun. It will indeed be amazing if we find Grace."

CHAPTER 10

Thursday, April 9, 1942
9:19 AM
Outside Springfield, Illinois

Bauer studied Alistar Fister as he consumed a huge breakfast. Based on his appetite and energy, the man appeared to be back to his old form. But how long would it last? How much time before his body began to fail in such a dramatic way there would be no coming back, regardless of how many injections he was given? As his guest polished off the last of his fried eggs, Bauer got up from the kitchen table and ambled back to his library. He loved this small room. It was filled with his favorite books and carefully coded research notes. When he tired of working, he read. When he tired of reading, he worked. This place kept his life in balance.

Walking between two high-backed Victorian chairs, like those usually seen in British gentlemen's clubs, he took his place behind a small walnut desk and scrutinized the only framed photograph in the entire house. The woman in the picture appeared to be in her early twenties. Though her look was pensive, her beauty all but leapt from behind the glass. Bauer's eyes misted as he traced her high cheekbones and moved over her full lips. Harlow, Garbo, Crawford, and even Colbert couldn't hold a candle to her. In his mind, this creature had been the most perfect woman ever to walk the earth.

"Who is she?" Fister asked from the doorway.

Bauer glanced up. "You must be feeling better; it seems you're light on your feet again. I'm guessing your cat-like reflexes are back too."

"I feel good," the man assured him as he took a seat near the room's entrance. "But you didn't answer my question."

Bauer paused, his eyes falling once more on the eight-by-ten, black-and-white image before forcing a slight smile. Leaning back in his chair, he sighed, folded his hands together in his lap, and shook his head. He gazed at the wooden-slant ceiling for several moments before breaking the silence.

"You ready to go back to work?"

"If you think I'm well enough. You know how much I hate this place. It's like being trapped. I need life and action to live."

"And the injections," Bauer added.

"How often?"

"I'm not sure. The three I've given you have seemingly brought you back to normal...or your version of normal. But how long will that last? You used to be able to go a few months between them, but now I believe we might have to increase the regimen to perhaps once a week. For the moment I think I can guarantee you'll be good until at least next Wednesday or so. That gives you plenty of time to get me a bit of much needed information. How would you like to go to Missouri?"

"My last trip through there was miserable. I walked more than I rode, and I didn't eat too well either."

"Well, you'll travel in style this time."

"What do I need to do?"

Bauer smiled "Just visit with a man who's looking for funding for a project. He's searching for something Hitler wants. Like most of his ideas, I think this one's crazy, but Hitler believes in the supernatural. He studies history for any signs that mystical relics from the past might still exist and offer him some kind of super power. He's actually looking for the Ark of the Covenant. Imagine that! A man bent on exterminating every Jew on the planet is lusting for their most sacred artifact. He's simply off his rocker."

"If you don't buy into his thinking, why chase what he wants?"

"Because I'm paid millions to do so. And when you have a fool willing to buy snake oil, you keep looking for more snake oil."

"So what's he after in Missouri?"

"There's a professor of history in Columbia who's been doing research on an early European trip to America. He might have a line on a lost map Hitler wants. The problem is, the researcher's out of money. He can't continue his studies, field trips, or digs without it. You're going to visit with him, let him tell you about his lifelong dream of finding this artifact, and then offer him the funding he needs to finish."

Fister grinned. "I'm guessing there's a catch."

"There always is, but he doesn't have to know that. Meanwhile, here's what you need to know. The man's name is Dr. Warren Williams. He's a bachelor, in his fifties, very eccentric, and completely devoted to his study of American history. He's short and stocky, wears thick glasses, and always looks as if he slept in his clothes. From what I've been told, he might just do that. But in this one case, he believes in what others feel is nothing but an ancient pipe dream…and that pipe dream is something Hitler desperately wants."

Bauer paused, pushed out of the chair, and crossed the room to look out onto the flat Illinois prairie. After jamming his hands into the pockets of his black slacks, he said, "If this map really exists, it'll get us millions in cash and jewels, and also some art treasures I'd love to claim as my own."

"Hitler would pay that much for a map?"

The tall man nodded. "And it would be worthless. That's what I like about doing favors for Hitler. He pays huge amounts for fables, while cutting corners in areas where he needs to be spending his money."

"Where does this map lead?"

Bauer turned to face Fister. "What do you know about the Spanish explorer Ponce De Leon?"

"He pretty much wasted his life looking for the Fountain of Youth."

"And as Ponce died at the age of forty-seven, I don't guess

he ever found it. But don't try to tell Hitler that."

"So Professor Williams believes in this legend?"

"I don't know about that," Bauer admitted, "but he believes there's a map that supposedly shows the way to what explorers thought was the Fountain of Youth. And all we need is that map. So I'll fund the research in order to get my hands on it as quickly as possible. I need to cash in before Hitler runs out of money. After all, it's Nazi money that's going to fund my postwar business."

"So I just go down to Missouri and offer him the money he needs?"

"Let's be a bit more sophisticated. You'll be a Scotsman named Riley O'Mally. You'll be representing the Antiquities Research Foundation. You explain that you're there to find out more about his research in this area and, if you're impressed, you'll award a grant to fund it."

"What if he decides to check it out? Won't he see it's a sham?"

"It's anything but a sham," Bauer assured him. "The ARF has been around for five years and has an office in Boston. And though it can't be traced to me, I own it."

The look on Fister's face made it obvious he was impressed. "How did you know to create that kind of business?"

"From the time he took power, I knew what Hitler lusted for. The key is knowing your customer. He believes in legendary mystical power. He thinks Germans descended from Norse gods. I don't know if he actually believes in God, but I'm pretty sure he thinks Satan is real. So founding the ARF to help me bilk the Fuhrer was just a logical move in setting the groundwork to gaining his trust."

"When do I leave?"

"I've already made the appointment for you. There's car in the barn, and you'll have documents proving who you are in an attaché case in the car's front seat. You need to be at Dr. Williams' office on Saturday at two-thirty in the afternoon. Spend a few hours with him, let him trot out his dog-and-pony show and bore you with all he's uncovered on this subject, then find out what his financial needs are and assure him the ARF will get it to him if he'll devote himself to nothing but this project over the next few months. Then come back here and I'll have the company deliver the money to him."

Bauer moved back to his desk, sat down, and crossed his arms over his chest. "Alistar, the clothes you need are in the lab. Emma can help you pack. You'll likely want to drive at least part of the way tonight. But once you complete your business, you'll need to get back here right away. I think the injection will keep you going well into next week, but you best not risk staying gone that long until we get a grip on the actual timetable."

"Okay," Fister said as he got up and turned toward the door. He was halfway through the room's lone entry when he paused and looked back to his host. "There's something you need to know."

Bauer grinned. "That you want to kill me for what I've done to you?"

"That thought has crossed my mind," Fister admitted.

"If you kill me, you'll kill yourself. I'm the only person

who can keep you going."

"Yeah. Now that I have all my faculties, I realize that. What I wanted you to know was that the cardboard tube I was supposed to take to Hitler..." He paused and nervously pushed his thumbs into his belt.

"Yes, Alistar, go ahead."

"Grace Lupino took it from me."

"So she has the two documents?"

"Yes. I'm sorry about that."

"I'm not. I figured you'd given them to the pilot who delivered Kranz to the U-boat captain, so I thought they'd gone down at sea. It's better they didn't. Now you go get ready for your mission."

After his guest left the house, Bauer put his feet up on the desk and smiled. Grace Lupino was shrewd and cunning. She knew she needed a bargaining chip and had bought herself some more time. How much more was for him to decide.

Bauer spun in his swivel chair, rose to his feet, and crossed the room to a large bookshelf. As he pulled out a volume of *Huckleberry Finn*, the left side of the case moved about an inch away from the wall. Pulling it forward revealed a staircase leading to a hidden basement. After switching on a light, Bauer descended the fifteen wooden steps. Once he arrived in the fifty-by-thirty-foot chamber, he grinned. Some of the greatest art treasures in the world, all of them looted by the Nazis during their European invasions, were here, as well as a countless fortune in gold and diamonds. And it was only the beginning. This was nothing more than the foundation of his collection.

Strolling to the back of the room, he reached out and switched on a floor lamp. There, sitting in a blue, velvet-covered chair that once adorned the bedroom of Marie Antoinette, was a woman. She was dressed in the finest clothing of another age, her dark hair carefully styled, with a large jeweled necklace that had once been the property of an oriental queen dangling around the lace collar that hugged her neck. She'd likely once been very beautiful, but those days were long passed; now she was only very dead.

The President's Service Series

Made in the USA
San Bernardino, CA
26 March 2017